DEEP IN THE BELLY OF THE MINE

Jessie raced for the steam engine at the other end of the catwalk. Buster let out a roar of rage and fired at her. She swerved and heard the slug whine past her left ear and strike one of the heavy iron stamping machines with a sharp metallic *clang*.

The stamp mill suddenly thundered into life and the noise drowned out the sound of Buster's pursuit as well as Jessie's ragged breathing. The noise would keep her from hearing his next move.

Jessie drew the double-barreled derringer from her jacket pocket. Just two shots. Her first shot missed him. His shot hit her in the right bicep, causing her to drop the gun. . . .

*Also in the LONE STAR series
from Jove*

WESLEY ELLIS

LONE STAR

AT CRIPPLE CREEK

JOVE BOOKS, NEW YORK

LONE STAR AT CRIPPLE CREEK

A Jove Book / published by arrangement with
the author

PRINTING HISTORY
Jove edition / February 1990

ISBN: 0-515-10242-3

Jove Books are published by The Berkley Publishing Group,
200 Madison Avenue, New York, New York 10016.
The name "JOVE" and the "J" logo
are trademarks belonging to Jove Publications, Inc.

PRINTED IN THE UNITED STATES OF AMERICA

10 9 8 7 6 5 4 3 2 1

Chapter 1

.

"Wake up, Jessie!"

When Jessie's eyes remained closed, Ki took hold of her shoulder and shook her gently. "Jessie!"

Her eyes opened, blinked, and then closed again.

"I know you didn't get much sleep on this trip," Ki said to her. "But if you don't wake up—and get up—and do both now, we're going to miss our Denver stop."

"Oh!" Jessie exclaimed and sat up straight in her seat as the whistle of the train on which she and Ki were riding sent a piercing blast of sound into the late afternoon air. "I'm sorry, Ki. Are we here, then?"

"Almost. I woke you a few minutes before we're due to pull into the station. I thought you might want to freshen up before we left the train."

"Such euphemisms we all use," Jessie murmured to herself and then stifled a yawn. "'Freshen up' indeed."

"Should I have asked you if you wanted to use the convenience room?"

"Another euphemism," Jessie said as she stood up. "I'm going to use the toilet," she announced in a voice loud enough to be heard throughout the Pullman car.

Her words caused a woman across the aisle from her to blush.

Jessie gave her a brilliant smile and then strode down the aisle, holding on to the seats as she went to keep her balance on the swaying train. A moment later she undid the buttons on the curtains enclosing the so-called "convenience room" and went inside.

Later, when she emerged from the small enclosure, she almost collided with the conductor, who was marching down the aisle and calling out, "Next stop, Denver! Denver is the next stop!"

She rejoined Ki, who was lifting their bags down from an overhead rack. Then both of them, carrying their luggage, made their way to the platform between the cars. They braced themselves as the train slowed, wheels grinding on the rails, sparks and soot flying from its smokestack to darken the June day, cinders flying up from the roadbed below.

Jessie patted her hair into place beneath the ostrich-plumed green hat she wore. The hat matched the color of her eyes and contrasted nicely with the paleness of her smooth skin. She stood there between the cars, an almost regal woman. Tall but not at all ungainly. Slender but not gaunt. Her figure was exquisitely feminine. Firm breasts which were provocatively evident even now beneath the long linen duster she wore to keep her clothes free of the dirt that was one of the less pleasant aspects of train travel. Flared hips below a narrow waist. Copper-colored hair which reached her shoulders and caught the light like a lovely net.

Ki, standing next to Jessie, was taller than most Eurasians, part of the legacy he had inherited from his American father. His body was compact and muscular. There was about him an aura of quiet strength kept under firm control, but readily available when needed. His hair, straight and black, was worn longer than was the current fashion among American men. His eyes had an Oriental cast. They bore clear witness to the Japanese blood that flowed in his veins.

He, too, wore a linen duster over his three-piece sack suit. It nearly hid the highly polished black shoes he wore. On his head was a black bowler.

As the train screeched to a sudden stop, the conductor reappeared. "Excuse me, please." He stepped down from the train, carrying a small step stool in his hand which he placed on the platform. He reached up, but Jessie declined his help. She stepped down onto the stool and from there to the platform.

She stood on the platform in the warm sun and looked about her. There were people hurrying in all directions, making her think of sheep when a wolf threatens the fold. She put down her luggage, and standing on the tips of her toes and using her hand to block the sun from her eyes, she continued searching the faces of the people around her.

"There," Ki said, and pointed.

Jessie looked at her left and saw Lavinia Carter, who was doing the same thing she had been doing, searching the faces of the people on the platform.

"Lavinia!" Jessie called out.

Lavinia turned, and when she saw Jessie waving to her, her eyes seemed to catch fire and a broad smile appeared on her face. She came running toward Jessie, and in an instant the two women were happily embracing.

"You look marvelous, my dear!" Lavinia cried, holding Jessie out at arm's length. Then, turning to Ki, she exclaimed, "And so do you, Ki, so do you." She gave him her cheek to kiss, and then she clasped her hands together

3

and said, "Oh, I am ever so glad to see you both. I cannot tell you how happy you've made me by coming to Laura's wedding."

"We wouldn't have missed it for the world," Jessie assured Lavinia.

"I told John that maybe we were taking you away from far more important matters by asking you to come all the way to Denver for the wedding."

"Not at all, Lavinia. Even if I had had other commitments when I received your invitation, I would have postponed them. But, as it happened, Ki and I were planning to make a trip to Cripple Creek next month. When we received your invitation, we simply moved our planned trip up by a few weeks. We'll be going to Cripple Creek when we leave here."

"You have, as I recall, mining interests there. Am I correct?"

"Yes, you are. Starbuck Enterprises owns the Empire Gold Mine in Cripple Creek."

"You're not experiencing any difficulties at the mine, I hope."

"No, it's really pretty much a routine trip. Although the last monthly report I received from Fred Bolan, who manages the mine, did mention the possibility of some labor trouble, but he wasn't specific concerning it. He said we could discuss it when I got there. But let's put aside all this talk about business. Tell me about Laura. She must be thrilled at the prospect of a brand-new life ahead of her."

"Oh, she is, she most definitely is, Jessie. But let's talk about that on our way to the house. The carriage is out in front of the station."

They made their way there, and Ki helped both women into the carriage, taking the seat facing them.

"Laura must be in a state," Jessie said as the carriage driver pulled away from the station. "Flustered, I mean."

4

Lavinia shook her head, her eyes twinkling. "She's not at all. One would think a girl got married every day of the week and twice on Sundays to watch Laura go about her business as cool as you please. It is I who have been in a state, Jessie, and that's a fact. I get ready to go out, and I can't find my gloves. I go calling of a Sunday afternoon and find I have left my cards at home. The last month has been a horror!"

Jessie smiled.

So did Ki as he said, "I've really been looking forward to seeing Laura again—and you and John, too, of course, Lavinia. It's been years since I last saw her."

"Well, she was away at school all those years when we visited one another. But now all that's behind her. Tomorrow she will become Mrs. Mason Canfield and . . ." Lavinia's words trailed away. She rummaged about in her reticule and came up with a lace-trimmed handkerchief which she used to dab at her eyes.

When Jessie placed a consoling hand on her forearm, she seemed to recover. With her spine straight and her head held high, she declared, "I can't face losing my daughter who has been the apple of my eye since the very moment she was born."

Lavinia was undone again, this time by a sob that escaped her lips.

"You know what they say," Jessie remarked, and Ki finished her statement by pointing out to Lavinia, "You're not losing a daughter, you're gaining a son."

"I know," Lavinia sniffed. Then, brightening, she added, "It should be a splendid affair tomorrow. Actually, I'm so looking forward to it. We are having Appleton's do the catering. We're expecting nearly a hundred guests at the wedding and reception. We've redecorated the ballroom for the occasion—white satin draperies, white tulle trim for the serving tables. We've imported calla lilies

5

from New York City, Reverend Fiskey is coming from St. Louis, where we were living when Laura was born to perform the service—he baptized her, you know—and . . ."

Jessie sat back in her seat as the carriage rolled along and, with Ki, listened to Lavinia's enthusiastic but somewhat disjointed account of all the plans that had been made for the wedding which would take place at eleven o'clock the next morning.

By the time they reached the Carter home, a three-story baroque structure with cupolas, gingerbread and latticework trim, and gables, Jessie and Ki had learned that the organist who would play at the wedding was named Percy Soames, that Lavinia was "simply terrified" that the calla lilies would begin to turn brown before the great day was over, that Laura's husband-to-be was a stockbroker in the renowned Denver firm of Hoskins, Barton, and Beame and that Laura hadn't the slightest doubt in her mind that her beloved Mason would be a partner in the firm within a year—two at the outside.

As the carriage came to a halt at the front door of the house, which was set back from the street on a vast property of smooth lawns dotted with mature boxwoods, Ki got out and helped the two women down from the carriage. Before any of them had reached the front door, it flew open and a beaming John Carter was coming toward them, his arms outstretched to embrace Jessie.

Then, shaking hands with Ki, he declared, "You look tiptop, the two of you, I must say. Jessie, if your father could see you now, he wouldn't know what to think. I'm sure he never thought he could have sired such a lovely young woman, the old codger. But I always knew you'd turn out to be a beauty. I told him so often enough. I told him he didn't know what he had done, unleashing a heartbreaker such as yourself on the unsuspecting men of the world."

"Oh, John, hush, you mustn't carry on so!" a smiling Lavinia admonished her husband.

"Do let him go on, Lavinia," Jessie said with a wink at Ki. "I absolutely adore such outrageous flattery. It quite delights me."

"Come inside," Carter said, ushering Jessie, Ki, and his wife into the house. "Bridget!" he called at the top of his voice.

When a round-faced maid wearing a black bombazine dress and a white apron appeared in the hall, he said, "Send Willian to fetch our guests' luggage."

"Yes, sir," Bridget said, and pertly curtsied. She disappeared for several minutes and then reappeared to announce, "William's gone to see to the luggage, Mr. Carter."

"Very good, Bridget. Now if you'll show Miss Starbuck and the gentleman with her to their rooms, please."

"Before you go," Lavinia said to her guests, "we were planning on having dinner at eight. Is that satisfactory to both of you? Yes? Very well. Laura will have returned from the hairdresser's by then, and Mason and his brother, Mitchell, will be joining us. Laura's aunt, John's sister from San Francisco, is staying here with us, as you both are, and she will be with us at dinner as well."

The clock on the fireplace mantel in Jessie's room read twenty minutes of eight as she stood in front of a large gilded mirror above her dressing table wearing only a chemise, pantalettes, and corset. She turned this way and that, critically eyeing her figure in the light from the lamp on her night table. She sat down in front of the mirror and leaned toward it. She picked up her bottle of rosewater and applied a drop to each earlobe and two to her throat. Then, picking up her powder puff, she lightly dusted her face.

Rising, she slipped into her silk petticoat and then her

yellow linen dress, which had a white lace collar and cuffs. She chose a simple mother-of-pearl brooch from among the items in her jewelry box and pinned it just below her collar. After pulling on her brown evening slippers, she again bent toward the mirror and bit both of her lips until they reddened. She was pinching her cheeks to bring a blush to them when there was a knock on her door.

She opened it to find Ki standing in the hall.

"You look quite handsome, sir," she told him. "I love the smell of the scent you're wearing."

"After-shave cologne," Ki corrected her.

"It smells like lilacs."

"It's called Lilac Vegetal. I'm told by my supplier back home that Edouard Pinaud, parfumeur to the court of Napoleon the Third, produced it for the contingent of Hungarian cavalry then attached to His Majesty's court."

"How very dashing. Shall we go downstairs?"

Jessie took Ki's arm and they went downstairs, where they found several people gathered in the dining room, Laura Carter among them.

When Laura saw Jessie in the doorway of the dining room, she let out a little cry and ran across the room to hug her friend.

"How very good of you to come, Jessie!" she cried, cheeks flushing with excitement. "Mother told me you had arrived. I want to thank you for coming. I want to thank you both for coming. How are you, Ki?"

"Fine, Laura. And you, I'm sure, must be nothing but wonderful."

"Oh, I am, Ki, I truly truly am! I am absolutely the luckiest woman in the world and I'll show you why. Come along, both of you!"

Laura, taking both Ki and Jessie by the hands, led them around the table to where a woman was standing with a glass of white wine held in her diamond-studded hand and a tall darkly handsome man was intently watching Jessie as he had been doing since she entered the dining room.

"Aunt Fancy," Laura said to the woman, "I'd like you to meet two very dear friends of mine. Jessica Starbuck and her friend, Ki. Jessie and Ki, my Aunt Fancy and my husband-to-be, Mason Canfield."

"At last I get to meet the renowned Jessica Starbuck in the flesh!" cried Fancy, her eyelashes flickering, the diamonds on her fingers flashing. "How do you do, my dear?"

"I'm quite well, Mrs.—Miss—"

"The name's Bristol. That was my fourth—and last, let me tell you—husband's name. But call me Fancy. That's not really my name, but it'll do."

"Aunt Fancy's real given name is Fanny," Laura volunteered.

"But when my niece was a very young child, she started calling me Fancy for the Lord alone knows why," Fancy put in with a deep-throated laugh. "Ki, you're the right-hand man of this beautiful creature, I'm told. It is a pleasure to meet you, sir."

"How do you do, Mrs.—"

"Fancy," Laura's aunt interrupted.

Ki nodded. "I'm pleased to meet you, Fancy."

"Mr. Canfield," Jessie said, offering her hand to Laura's fiancé.

"Miss Starbuck," he said, not shaking her hand but instead taking it and bending low to kiss it. "Please call me Mason."

"I shall if you'll call me Jessie."

Canfield gave Jessie a pleased smile before turning to shake hands with Ki.

"I told mother she shouldn't invite you to the wedding, Jessie," Laura suddenly stated.

9

"Not invite me—why ever not?"

"I didn't want Mason to see you."

"You didn't want— I'm afraid I don't understand."

"I was afraid that once he saw how beautiful you are, he'd never look at me again."

The others joined in Laura's self-deprecating laughter.

"May I know what the joke is?"

Jessie turned to find a man as darkly handsome as Mason Canfield standing just behind her.

"You must be Jessie," he said. "John told me you had arrived today for the wedding. I'm pleased to make your acquaintance."

Jessie. Not Miss Starbuck. The man moves right in, Jessie thought, not minding at all.

"I'm Mitchell Canfield, Mason's brother. But not nearly as fortunate as he is because, as you know"—Mitchell put a companionable arm around Laura's shoulders and hugged her to him— "this charming creature has spurned me in favor of my younger brother."

"That's not true, Mitchell," Laura protested. "I'd never spurn you. We'll be friends forever, you and I."

Mitchell assumed a forlorn expression and spread out his hands in a gesture of helplessness. "Now you see, Jessie, that what I just told you is all too true. Mason is the fortunate sibling in the Canfield household. *He* is going to marry Laura. I am to be merely her friend forever. A sad state of affairs, I must say. But then turnabout's fair play, isn't it? Perhaps I should now spurn Laura in favor of you, Jessie."

Jessie, feeling heat in her cheeks, silently damned herself for blushing. To cover her momentary discomfiture, she introduced Mitchell Canfield to Ki.

The two men were shaking hands and exchanging pleasantries when John and Lavinia Carter entered the dining room.

"I see we're all here," Lavinia observed. "I'll tell the

servants we're ready for dinner, shall I?" Without waiting for an answer, Lavinia left the room.

Ki was about to offer to escort Jessie to the table, but Mason Canfield did so first.

Placecards directed Jessie to a seat to the right of John Canfield, who sat at the head of the table which gleamed with crystal candelabra in which beeswax tapers burned brightly. Across from her was Lavinia and on her right was Mitchell Canfield. Mason was seated next to Lavinia on the other side, and on his left was Ki, who faced Laura, who had taken her place on Mitchell's right. Opposite John Canfield was Aunt Fancy.

Servants appeared from the kitchen, and Jessie soon found a small bowl of aspic containing baby shrimp and diced lobster on her serving plate.

"I hate aspic," Mitchell whispered to her in a low tone.

She gave him a quizzical glance.

"Can't keep the stuff on my spoon," he exclaimed *sotto voce*.

Jessie suppressed a giggle.

"Jessie," Fancy said from her seat at the end of the table. "Do tell us about your most recent adventures—the ones you've shared with Ki. I've read about some of them in the newspapers, and I even heard rumors concerning your derring-do when I was in London last year."

"I'd really rather not," Jessie demurred. "I'd much rather hear from Laura about the plans she and Mason have made for their honeymoon."

"Oh, but I insist," Fancy declared, refilling the wine glass she had just emptied. "I adore hearing about gunfights and villains and handsome men coming to your rescue when all seems lost. Weren't you involved in some sort of nasty business in Indian Territory? Something to do with the deaths of some of your employees?"

"The men who were herding some Starbuck Enterprises

cattle north to grazing lands we lease in Indian Territory, yes. The men were murdered."

"Murdered!" Fancy exclaimed in a shocked but interested tone. She emptied her glass. "How *appalling*!"

"Where did you and Mason plan to spend your honeymoon?" Jessie asked Laura as the bowl that had contained her aspic was withdrawn and a plate containing broiled trout with a slice of lemon adorning it was set before her.

"We're going to Aspen," Laura replied with a fond glance at Mason. "We both love the mountains."

"Who murdered them?" Fancy interjected and hiccuped.

"It's a rather long story," Jessie replied. "I don't think this is the time or place to go into it."

Fancy's face fell. Thrusting out her lower lip, she pouted. Then, with a shrug, she drank some more wine and said, "I envy you, darling. I truly do. I have so little excitement in my own life these days."

"How can you say that, Aunt Fancy?" Laura asked. "Why, when you were in New York last month you told us a fortune hunter nearly swindled you out of thousands of dollars."

"He said he wanted to marry me," Fancy declared airily and a bit wistfully. "But I was on to him right from the start. He called himself J. Robert Swanson. But when I handed him over to the police, it turned out that they knew him as Bad Jack Mishkin, who made his way in the world by wooing and marrying and then deserting lonely women. Lonely women of means, I should add. He robbed them of their worldly assets and then vanished, never to be seen nor heard from again. As one's youth does."

"You were lucky to escape the dastardly fellow's clutches," John Carter proclaimed stentoriously.

Fancy put down her empty wineglass. "But I didn't, John, dear. Escape his clutches, I mean. Nor did I want to. Bad Jack—or J. Robert Swanson, as he pretended to me he was named—was quite a man. In the clutches."

Ki guffawed.

Laura blushed.

Lavinia looked down at her plate.

John busied himself with his trout.

Mason and Mitchell Canfield exchanged glances as Jessie patted her lips with her napkin to prevent the laughter that was bubbling up inside her from escaping.

"Oh, don't look so scandalized, Lavinia," Fancy said. "You know I always tell the truth. Would that more people did the same. We would have less chaos in the world if they did, though, admittedly, a lot of shocked people into the bargain."

Turning her attention to Jessie once more, she continued, "I'll bet you've run into a man or two in your time who was as good in the clutches as my Bad Jack was before I turned him over to the law and went looking for greener pastures—not to mention another man."

Jessie glanced at Ki, who raised his eyebrows in expectation of her answer.

"Fancy, you're asking me to kiss and tell, something I never do."

"Good response!" a pleased Fancy exclaimed. "We girls should keep our conquests to ourselves lest the easily scandalized—present company definitely *not* excluded—should banish us from polite society."

Fancy then proceeded to regale those at the table with a rambling account of her recent visit to Morocco, where, she said, she rode a camel for the first—and last—time in her life and would have loved to have been able to bring home with her the eighteen-year-old Arab with whom she had enjoyed what she called a "lovely liaison," but she feared she wouldn't have been able to get him through customs without paying an exorbitant duty since, she said, he had cost her nearly several thousands of dollars in fees

13

"for services rendered." Her raucous laughter bounded about the table as the others ate their just-served dessert—cherries jubilee—and she continued to sip from her wineglass.

After dinner the diners retired to the music room, where cognac and demitasse were served.

"Play something for us, Mason," Mitchell urged. "Your bride-to-be can sing along with you."

"Oh, yes, please do," Lavinia pleaded. "They perform so beautifully together," she confided to Jessie.

Fancy let out a burst of ribald laughter. "I shouldn't think you'd want to admit to such a thing," she told Lavinia with a wink. "After all, they're not yet married."

Lavinia, nonplussed, gave a sigh of despair over her sister-in-law's bawdiness.

Mason sat down at the piano and Laura joined him. As he began to play "Down a Country Lane," one of the day's popular songs, Laura sang the lyrics.

Jessie listened, keenly conscious of Mitchell Canfield seated beside her on a sofa. She felt the warmth of his body next to hers. Or was she feeling, she wondered idly, only the warmth his presence aroused in her own body? She tried to concentrate on the words of the song Laura was singing so beautifully. Something about shadows and sunlight. Something about it being true. . . .

"Is it true?" Mitchell whispered to her a second time.

She hadn't been hearing the words of the song. She had been hearing Mitchell's whispered words. "Is what true?" she asked him.

"That you're an adventuress, as Aunt Fancy seems to think." He didn't wait for an answer. "An adventuress would agree to share a bottle of champagne with me at Benedetto's. That's a cozy little bistro in town."

"I can't accept on the grounds that my acceptance may tend to incriminate me."

14

"Your refusal to accept would suggest to me a distinct and deplorable lack of courage."

"Must a woman possess courage to accompany you to Benedetto's?"

"Touché." Mitchell moved closer to Jessie. "What's it to be? Benedetto's for both of us or a broken heart for me?"

Jessie couldn't help herself. She smiled. The man was decidedly and, she strongly suspected, deliberately melodramatic. But he was also very attractive. "I wouldn't want you to suffer a broken heart."

"Ah, an angel of mercy." Mitchell broke into a broad smile. "Let's excuse ourselves and leave right now."

"No, not right now. That would be impolite."

"You mean we mustn't eat and run."

"I haven't given Laura and Mason my wedding present. Excuse me for a moment."

Jessie rose as Laura finished her song to polite applause from her listeners. She went over to where Ki was sitting and spoke softly to him. She waited then as he excused himself and left the room.

When he returned a few minutes later, a bridge game was in progress with Laura and Mason playing against John and Lavinia.

Fancy had slipped into sleep on a brocaded chaise longue, her arms flung wide as she softly snored. Mitchell was pacing the room impatiently, his eyes pleading silently with Jessie, who was trying her best but failing to ignore him.

Ki gave the smaller of the two brightly wrapped and gaily beribboned packages he was carrying to Jessie, who excused herself for interrupting the card game and then handed it to Laura.

Laura thanked her and hurriedly removed the ribbon and wrapping from the package. She exclaimed in delight over the French porcelain fruit compote the box contained. She

15

picked it up by its large gilded handles and held it up for all to see.

"Look at the cherubs!" she cried, referring to the two winged figures supporting the bowl as they knelt on its ornate base. "Thank you, Jessie. It's just lovely. I shall treasure it and think of you every time I use it."

Ki stepped forward and gave his wedding gift to Laura, which turned out to be a phonograph that reproduced sound which had been recorded on a tin-foil cylinder.

"Oh, how marvelous!" Laura exclaimed, clapping her hands. "Look, Mason. It's one of Mr. Edison's recent inventions."

"Thank you both very much," Mason said to Jessie and Ki. "We appreciate your thoughtfulness."

"More cognac, Jessie?" John Carter inquired, holding high a crystal decanter which sparkled in the lamplight.

Before Jessie could respond, Mitchell said, "John, you're stealing my thunder."

"I beg your pardon?"

"I'm taking Jessie on a late-night tour of the city, and I've promised to take her to Benedetto's for champagne afterward. More cognac would surely spoil her palate."

"I see. Very well. There's a nearly full moon tonight. A drive through the city will be quite lovely, I'm sure."

"Romantic, too," Ki whispered to Jessie as she began to say her good-nights.

"We'll see you both in the morning," Lavinia said as she walked with Jessie and Mitchell to the front door.

"Watch your step!" Fancy was sitting up on her chaise and yawning as she pointed a finger at Mitchell. "He may be a fortune hunter, darling," she teased. "He may be after the Starbuck Enterprises empire. Be very wary of such dashing young men. They might steal you blind."

Jessie laughed with Fancy and then she and Mitchell went outside into the soft summer night.

He put his arm around her waist as he led her to his carriage, which was parked in the driveway of the house. "It's not your business empire I intend to steal tonight," he whispered in her ear. "It's your heart."

Jessie felt desire flow hotly through her as Mitchell bent down and gently kissed her cheek.

They spent less than ten minutes driving through Denver before Mitchell drew rein in front of Benedetto's, which had gas lamps burning on either side of its carved mahogany door.

Jessie was about to alight from the carriage when he caught her wrist. As she turned toward him, he said, "I suddenly seem to have lost my taste for champagne. But if you really want some—"

Leaving his sentence unfinished, Mitchell leaned over and put an arm around Jessie. "This is what I have a taste for." He kissed her lips, his mouth open, his tongue probing.

Jessie was left gasping when he withdrew from her. "I've never really liked champagne all that much," she murmured breathlessly.

Mitchell grinned as he pulled away from the curb.

"Where are we going?" Jessie asked as they drove in and out of yellow pools of gaslight that illumined the street.

"Home."

"You're taking me back to the Carters?" she asked incredulously.

He shook his head. "Not on your life. We're going to *my* home. I rent a suite of rooms at the Garfield Hotel."

Ten minutes later they arrived at the hotel, and five minutes after that Mitchell was unlocking his door and escorting Jessie into a modestly furnished living room.

"Would you like something to drink?" he asked her.

"No, nothing, thank you." She stood with her back to

the door Mitchell had just locked looking at him, appraising his slender but muscular body, his lean face that was blued by the faint shadow of a beard. He was a very desirable man, she decided as she walked over to a loveseat and sat down, spreading her arms out across its back.

He came over and sat down beside her. He cradled her face in his hands and his lips lightly touched hers. She moved closer to him, her right arm leaving the sofa to draw him to her. She felt his tongue slide between her parted lips. She moaned faintly as she began to suck on it.

Mitchell lifted her to her feet. She felt the hardness of his body pressing against her own. She felt his hands roaming over her body and sending shivers of delight and desire coursing through her.

"The bedroom," he murmured as he took her by the hand and led her into it.

Chapter 2

Mitchell helped Jessie undress. Soon her pantalettes, chemise, and corset had joined her dress on a chair in a corner of the bedroom.

As she lay down on the huge bed that dominated the room, he hurriedly undressed, practically tearing the clothes from his body in his haste to join her.

When he did so a moment later, he immediately began to fondle her breasts, his hand running down her rib cage past her navel to come to rest against her hot and already moist mound. As he cupped it in one eager hand, he grew even harder than he already was. He rolled over on top of Jessie, and as he did so she threw her head back and her right hand slid between their bodies.

He groaned with pleasure as he felt her fingers close on his rigid shaft. He arched his back and raised his pelvis slightly in order to give her more room to maneuver.

She surprised him by sliding out from under him and forcing him down upon the bed, where he stared up at her with lustful eyes. She straddled him, and then she was sliding down along his body until she was kneeling between his legs.

He moaned and closed his eyes as she lowered her head and took him into her mouth. He lay there, luxuriating in the sensations she was causing to flood through his entire body as her head rose and fell, rose and fell upon him in a rhythm that almost brought him to a climax.

But then, as if she had known how close to coming he was, Jessie suddenly released him and skillfully maneuvered her body until she had mounted him. Settling down on him, taking his entire length into her, she swiveled her hips, first this way, then that.

He opened his eyes and saw the faint smile on her face.

"You're—you're—" He searched for the word, the right word that would define what she was to him at that moment. It never came to him, lost as he was in a sea of sensations that were raging within him as Jessie bucked wildly above his quivering body.

He raised his head and took her left breast in his mouth. His tongue flicked over its nipple. His lips suckled. He moved to her right breast and repeated the process. He felt himself about to explode . . .

But Jessie again slowed her movements while keeping him locked within her and his climax did not occur. Then, moving slowly but with a kind of fierce intensity, she began again to bring him to the point where he would find release. She kept at it until he was nearly maddened by the sensations she was stirring to a fever pitch within him. Each time—and there were four in all—she brought him to the brink and then eased him back from it.

The fifth time she brought him to a climax that caused his entire body to shudder so violently it shook the bed despite their combined weight pressing down upon it. A moment after he had flooded her, she, too, climaxed, giving as she did so a series of little cries interspersed with grunts of pure pleasure. Her head was thrown back, her long hair hanging down behind her, her lips parted, and her skin glistening with a sheen of sweat.

Mitchell was able only to moan with pleasure at first, but then, as his body stilled somewhat and Jessie lay down beside him on the bed, he turned to her and said, "It would seem"—he paused to catch his breath—"someone has taught you to make love in a way I never would have thought possible. You've left me limp in more ways than one—but mind you, I'm not complaining."

She touched his lips with the tip of her right index finger. "If you found me an expert practitioner of the art of love, that was because you are a very desirable man and I wanted to give you as much pleasure as I could."

"It's that you did, my dear, that you most certainly and unmistakably did indeed. Were I a magician, I could not have conjured up a more wonderful woman to warm my heart." He kissed the tip of her finger.

"Was it only your heart I warmed?"

He parried her teasing remark with "Forget my heart for the moment. What you warmed almost melted from the heat of your fire."

"Now that would be a shame if that happened. I shall have to be more careful next time."

"Don't you dare be careful!" Mitchell cried, and laughing, embraced her.

The next time they coupled a few minutes later, Jessie was not at all careful, making Mitchell a happy man as he gladly burned in the fire her desire for him had once again kindled within him.

Jessie awoke the next morning in her room in the Carters' home with a faint smile on her face, the direct result of her pleasant dreams about the previous night's lovemaking with Mitchell Canfield. She squirmed under the silk sheet that covered her, stretching to loosen and limber her sleep-sodden body.

It had been, she thought, quite a night. Quite a wonderful night. She could still feel Mitchell's hard body pressing down upon her own, feel his hard— Her smile broadened.

There was a knock on the bedroom door, interrupting her reverie.

She rose and pulled her dressing gown over her night-dress. "I'm coming."

She opened the door to find Lavinia, fully dressed, standing in the hall, a folded newspaper in her hand.

"Did I wake you, dear?" her hostess asked solicitously.

"No. I was awake, but I'm afraid I should have been up and about much earlier." Then, seeing the strained expression on Lavinia's face, she asked, "What is it? Is something wrong?"

"I'm afraid so."

"Come in."

When Lavinia was inside the bedroom and seated in a chair, Jessie sat down on the bed and asked, "What's bothering you, Lavinia?"

"This." Lavinia held up the newspaper.

Jessie looked quizzically at it and then at Lavinia, an unspoken question in her expression. She took the paper Lavinia was holding out to her.

"The front page," Lavinia said. "Near the bottom."

Jessie unfolded the newspaper and scanned the front page. The story leaped out at her, the one headlined:

ATTEMPTED MURDER
IN CRIPPLE CREEK

Quickly she began to read.

The law-abiding citizens of this prosperous mining community were shocked yesterday to learn that one of their own, Mr. Frederick Bolan, General Manager of the Empire Gold Mine, was shot and seriously wounded in the left arm by an unknown assailant. Mr. Bolan had just finished his day's work at the mine, which is owned by a business conglomerate with a world-wide reputation, Starbuck Enterprises, and which has been suffering as a result of a strike called by Mr. Dan Calhoun.

Mr. Bolan was treated at Mercy Hospital for what doctors described as a wound involving not only torn flesh but also broken bone. Mr. Bolan is expected to recover fully, but his doctor warns that his recovery will take some time.

When questioned about the motive for the attack upon him, Mr. Bolan declared, "It undoubtedly has something to do with our operation's unwillingness to submit to the outrageous wage demands being made upon us by the leader of the strikers, Mr. Dan Calhoun. Such irresponsible individuals will stop at nothing— not even, apparently, violence—to win their way."

Mr. Calhoun subsequently denied any knowledge of the shooting and disavowed it completely, calling it "an outrage but readily understandable under the circumstances." When pressed to explain what he meant, Mr. Calhoun said that "desperate men will perform desperate acts, and we have a lot of desperate men on strike here in Cripple Creek. They have been made desperate by the terrible conditions under which they were being forced to work, and they have also been made desperate by the fact that the mine owners are almost criminally unconcerned with the men who have helped them amass their enormous fortunes. They care no more for their workers than they would for a cur they cruelly kick out of their path."

Mr. Bolan said that he fully expects more trouble to erupt at the Empire Mine and at other struck gold mines in the area during the current strike. He said he intends to take what he called "appropriate steps" to defend himself. He admitted under further questioning that there have been threats made against the management of other mines to be carried out if the workers' demands are not met. "I will not be intimidated," Mr. Bolan said.

Jessie felt like cheering Fred Bolan for the firm stand he had taken in the face of what was apparently very real danger. There was more to the story and she read it all. It basically recapitulated what had already been written. There was trouble in Cripple Creek between the miners and the mine owners. Serious trouble that was building up a strong head of steam (in the colorful words of the newspaper's reporter) and threatening to "explode at any moment."

"John thought you should see that article right away," Lavinia said. "He always likes to read the paper with his first cup of coffee in the morning. He asked me to give it to you. It sounds simply awful, doesn't it?"

Jessie didn't hear the question. Her thoughts were racing. Who was this Dan Calhoun? He was, according to the newspaper, the leader of the strikers. Had he also been behind the shooting of Fred Bolan despite his quoted denial? She didn't know, but she intended to find out and she intended to find out fast.

Anger replaced the anxiety she had been feeling as she read the newspaper story about the shooting of her mine's manager.

"You'll want to go to Cripple Creek as soon as possible," Lavinia was saying. "No, my dear, don't say anything. I understand the situation perfectly. I know we planned on having a longer visit with you and Ki, but that was before any of us knew about that." She pointed to the newspaper in Jessie's hand.

"We'll stay for the wedding. But then I think we should take the first train we can get to Cripple Creek."

"There is one leaving this afternoon. That means you'll miss the reception, but that can't be helped."

"If you'll excuse me, Lavinia, I want to show this story to Ki."

"Of course."

Both women rose and headed for the door. As Jessie opened it and they stepped out into the hall, she said, "After this trouble at Cripple Creek is over, we'll come back here and spend a few days with you and John as we originally planned to do."

"Oh, that will be wonderful. We'll be looking forward to your return."

Jessie left Lavinia and made her way to the door of Ki's room. When he opened it in response to her knock, he was wearing a nightshirt and slippers.

"We'll be leaving for Cripple Creek this afternoon," Jessie announced.

Ki's eyes widened in surprise. "I thought we were staying on here for several more days."

Jessie entered the room and closed the door behind her. "We were but our plans have just changed. Because of this." She handed him the newspaper.

"I don't understand."

"Read the story at the bottom of the first page."

Ki's brow furrowed as he read the account of the shooting at Cripple Creek. He sat down when he had finished reading and looked up at Jessie. "You'd been expecting trouble at the Empire Mine," he pointed out to her. "That's part of the reason you decided to go there."

"I wasn't expecting the shooting kind of trouble, though."

"Fred Bolan's last report suggested that labor trouble was brewing."

"Labor trouble, yes. But, as I just said, not the kind of trouble that would lead to a strike or an attempt on Fred Bolan's life."

"Whoa!" Ki said, holding the newspaper up in front of him as if he were fending off an attack. "I'm not the troublemaker. You don't have to yell at me."

"Was I yelling?"

"Like a woman wronged."

"I'm sorry. I didn't mean to make a scene. It's just that I'm upset. Fred Bolan could have been killed."

"But he wasn't."

"His wound is serious. The doctor said so. Bones in his arm were broken by the bullet somebody fired at him."

"There you go again."

"Yelling?"

"Yelling."

Jessie began to pace the room, her arms folded across her chest, a grim expression on her face. "I'm not just upset. It's more than that. Much more. I'm angry. Furious, as a matter of fact." She turned to face Ki. "Did you read the things Dan Calhoun, whoever he is, had to say in response to the attempt on Fred's life?"

"I read them, yes."

"The man sounds insufferable."

"Most men do when they've got an axe to grind."

"Do you think that's what it is with this man, Calhoun?"

"It would seem that way. He seems to be a spokesman, perhaps a self-appointed one, for the striking miners.

26

What's more, he seems to think they, the miners, have serious grievances against the owners."

"What grievances? I've always paid the men who work the Empire a decent wage. I've always insisted that the conditions under which they work be made as safe as humanly possible. Based on that newspaper account, it sounds as if the miners, having gained the moon, now want the sun as well. And Dan Calhoun appears ready and willing to try to get it for them. Well, he has reckoned without me."

"You intend, I gather, to take the man down a peg or two."

"I do indeed. I would be less than responsible were I not to stand up in defense of Fred Bolan and my own business practices."

"Jessie, I don't want to get you upset again, but I feel I have to point this out to you. It seems to me that you're getting things a bit mixed up. You're talking about Fred Bolan being shot and Dan Calhoun as if he were the shooter, all in the same breath. You don't know who shot Bolan. You don't know exactly what the problem—or problems, as the case may be—are in the mines at Cripple Creek. Until you do, I'd recommend a more judicious and temperate approach to this whole matter."

"Judicious! Temperate! You talk to me about being judicious and temperate when my business interests are threatened and my mine manager has been grievously wounded? Ki, I don't think you're being realistic about this."

"I happen to think I am. There is an old Japanese saying that I always thought made a good deal of sense. 'The man who would conquer the world must first know the facts that make up the world.'"

Jessie, fuming, went to the window and stood there looking out in silence for a long moment, her back to Ki.

Then, turning around, she said, "You infuriate me. You know that, don't you?"

Ki assumed an expression of utter innocence. "I do?"

Jessie began to tap her foot. "Yes, you do. What's more, you do so because nine times out of ten you are absolutely right in your advice, as I believe you are once again in this instance."

Ki said nothing, waiting for Jessie to continue.

"I shall go to Cripple Creek and I shall ascertain the facts and when I know them I will act."

"A commendable position to take."

"It is based on an old American saying: 'Once you know your enemy, go on the attack.'"

"Come on now, Jessie. You just made that supposed American saying up on the spur of the moment and out of thin air."

"I admit it. But I submit to you, it's as good as your Japanese saying."

"I submit to you that I made that one up, too, on the spur of the moment and out of thin air."

"You didn't."

"I did."

Both Jessie and Ki suddenly burst into loud laughter, which quickly dissipated the tension between them.

At eleven o'clock that morning, the wedding of Laura Carter and Mason Canfield took place in the sumptuously decorated ballroom of the Carter home. Jessie, with Ki by her side, surveyed the large room and came away with the pleasant impression of a summer garden in full and bright bloom based on the brilliant colors displayed in the gowns of the women present. Yellows, blues, greens, and orchids were the colors of the happy day, alongside which the men who were clad in much more somber blacks and grays and whites looked to her to be positively dull.

Her heart beat a little faster as the organist engaged for the occasion began to play the familiar Wedding March, which she recognized as being a part of the incidental music written for Shakespeare's *A Midsummer Night's Dream* by the great composer, Felix Mendelssohn.

"Doesn't she look lovely?" Jessie whispered to Ki as Laura, a bouquet of lilies of the valley in one hand and her other hand resting on the arm of her father, appeared in the doorway of the ballroom.

"Ravishing," Ki declared. "But John looks like he's about to walk his last mile."

"The father of the bride never looks happy at his daughter's wedding, I've always noticed."

"The mother of the bride doesn't look overjoyed, either."

Jessie glanced at Lavinia seated in the front of the room where the minister, black book in hand, stood waiting. Lavinia Carter sat with tears streaming down her face while, paradoxically, smiling.

"Their little girl isn't their little girl anymore, Ki," Jessie commented.

Heads turned to watch as Laura and her father made their way between the rows of guests. Eyes followed their progress toward Mason Canfield, who stood near the clergyman, his eyes on the lovely Laura, whose white satin gown shimmered in the sunlight streaming through the windows.

"Lucky man, Mason," Ki observed. "Which reminds me. Did you enjoy your late-night ride with Mason's best man?"

Jessie's gaze shifted from Laura to Mitchell Canfield, who was standing tall and stately beside his brother. "Yes, it was most enjoyable."

"It's too bad we're cutting our visit short. You haven't

really had much of a chance to get to know Mitchell Canfield."

"Oh, I've gotten to know him well enough," Jessie responded with the ghost of a smile playing across her face. "I'm sorry I haven't had a chance to tell him we'll be leaving right after the ceremony, but I asked Lavinia to tell him we would be returning here for a stay of a few days once matters are settled in Cripple Creek. When we do return, I expect I shall have ample opportunity to see Mitchell again—and get to know him even better than I do at present."

"Dearly beloved," intoned the clergyman, opening his book as John Carter handed his daughter over to Mason Canfield and the pair took up a side-by-side position in front of the minister. "We are gathered here together this day to unite in holy matrimony this man and this woman."

The rest passed in a blur for Jessie. There were more solemn words. There were the vows spoken firmly, indeed eagerly, by both Laura and Mason. There was more stirring organ music. And then there was the storm of congratulations from the well-wishers showered on the beaming bride and groom.

"Let's say good-bye," Jessie suggested to Ki. "Then we can get our luggage and leave."

"I've taken care of our luggage. It's already in the carriage's boot, and there's a driver waiting to take us to the station."

Jessie and Ki worked their way through the crowd of guests until they were facing Laura and Mason.

"Mr. and Mrs. Mason Canfield," Jessie began, "I want to wish you the best of everything, a wish, I assure you, that comes from the bottom of my heart."

Laura embraced Jessie and then Jessie embraced Mason.

"The very best to you both," Ki said, giving Laura a

30

polite kiss on the cheek and shaking Mason's hand.

"We're so sorry you both have to leave us so suddenly," Laura said.

"I promised your mother," Jessie said, "that we'd be back once our business in Cripple Creek is brought to a successful conclusion. "You'll be back from your honeymoon by that time, and you can tell us all about it then."

Someone threw a handful of rice, which interrupted the good-byes. When a laughing Laura and Mason recovered from the felicitous onslaught, Jessie and Ki were gone.

Jessie, as she sat in the window seat next to Ki on the train to Cripple Creek that afternoon, was wearing jeans tucked into black boots and a blue cotton blouse under her denim jacket. A flat-topped black Stetson sat on her lap. In the right pocket of her jacket rested a double-barreled derringer.

Ki now wore, not his three-piece sack suit, but jeans, battered black boots, a brown bib shirt, and a cordovan leather vest.

As the train rounded a curve, he absently took from his vest pocket one of the eight *shuriken* he always carried and began to twirl it in his fingers. The deadly Japanese throwing star had five blades sharp enough to bite deeply into wood. His index finger began to slide back and forth over the *shuriken*'s pintle hole, which was used to dispense the weapon during rapid-fire throws.

Anyone observing him would probably have assumed that he was daydreaming with his eyes wide open. But such was definitely not the case. He was instead focusing his life force, his *ki*, on the inward *tai-ten*, the "one point," as he sought and found a feeling of strength and a sense of being at the very center of the universe.

But his sense of serenity, of being as strong and power-

31

ful as any ten men, suddenly evaporated as the sound of a woman weeping seeped through the Pullman coach.

He turned and looked toward the rear of the coach from which the sound had come. He saw a woman standing near the door of the coach, but he could not see her face because her hands covered it as she stood—no, he thought, she's not standing, she's cowering—in front of the train's conductor. But he could see her figure, which he found enticing. She was, he estimated, about five and a half feet tall. Her figure was womanly in every respect. Wide hips. Narrow waist and shoulders. Breasts in full flower beneath the confines of the muslin dress she wore, which was imprinted with a pattern of tiny flowers in blue and green.

"What's the matter?" Jessie asked.

Ki didn't hear her because at the moment she had asked her question, the woman had taken her hands away from her tear-stained face to stare up in apparent fear at the conductor, who was still looming over her.

A beauty, Ki thought. Look at those blue eyes of hers. They're like beacons. Her skin's like silk, almost translucent, with a faint pink flush on each cheek. She's got herself a pert and pretty pair of lips that would be a pleasure to kiss and hair the color of honey. A melodic voice.

But what was she saying? And in what language was she saying it? She certainly wasn't speaking English.

"Ki, I asked you what's the matter back there."

"There's a young woman who seems to be having some kind of trouble with the conductor. She seems to be on the losing end of the matter. The problem is, it seems, she doesn't speak English. Excuse me, Jessie, I'll go and see if I can help her out."

Ki got up and walked down the aisle until he reached the woman and the conductor. "May I be of service, miss?"

The woman looked at him with fright-filled eyes as if he

were another enemy come to join forces with the conductor against her.

He put out a hand, and she gave a little cry and backed away from him.

"She's one of the Bohunks," the conductor announced with thinly disguised contempt.

"I'm afraid I don't follow you, sir," Ki said.

"They're traveling on the train. Got a car to themselves that's not much better than a cattle car." Sudden raucous laughter from the conductor. "Of course, that makes sense when you come to think of it. I mean these people aren't all that far removed from cattle themselves, are they?" His laughter degenerated into a fit of coughing.

Ki seized the moment to ask the woman where her seat was. When he got no response from her other than a petrified stare, he patted the seat next to him and then pointed at the woman.

She looked at the seat, at him, and shook her head.

"You don't know?" he prompted. "You don't know where your seat is?"

She shook her head, and Ki thought it a pretty gesture which on any other woman would have seemed merely ordinary.

"The Bohunks' car is at the end of the train," the conductor interjected when his coughing fit ended. "I started to march her back to it when she practically had hysterics on me."

"Thank you for your interest in the problem, conductor," Ki said politely, suppressing the urge to slam a fist into the man's fat mouth. "I'll take the lady to her accommodations."

Speaking softly though saying very little of import as one does when one wants to gentle a skittish horse or other edgy animal, Ki opened the door leading to the narrow platform between the cars. He beckoned to the woman, careful not to touch her.

She glanced at the conductor, who made chicken-shooing motions with both of his large hands. Then she looked at Ki, who continued to beckon to her. She opted to follow Ki, more, he speculated, to escape the conductor, who obviously terrified her, than because she had any great faith in him.

He opened the door to the next car, and she stepped through it. Progress, he thought, and gave her a reassuring smile. Walking backward, he made his way down the aisle of the coach they had just entered, still talking to the woman, still making what he hoped were soothing sounds.

She followed him, taking tiny tentative steps and glancing backward over her shoulder as if she feared pursuit by the conductor.

They finally moved into the third car. It was like entering Bedlam. Men were shouting. A baby was wailing. A cageful of chickens were cackling, their combed heads thrust through the bars of their wicker prison, their beaks agape. A dog barked, a rumbling sound like distant thunder.

"Lena!"

The man who had shouted burst out of the middle of a crowd of other men, all of them roughly dressed in tweeds and linsey-woolsey, and came rushing toward the woman Ki had just escorted into their presence.

He was a big man, a burly man, all shoulders and strong stocky limbs with a full beard covering most of his face. His black eyes burned with emotion, and his hamlike hands reached for the woman standing beside Ki, whom he had called Lena.

Ki wasn't sure what to do as the man came hurtling toward the woman. Was he about to attack her? Was it rage that blazed in the man's eyes? Ki took a step forward, bracing himself for a possible battle, but then he relaxed and even began to feel a bit foolish as the bear of a man took the woman in his arms, hugging and kissing her while fat tears leaked from his eyes and ran down the hills of his cheeks.

The pair parted and each of them began to talk to the other, using foreign words Ki had no hope of understanding. The man patted the woman's cheek. He rolled his eyes heavenward as if in thanksgiving. He did a little dance, twirling the woman about and making her skirt fly.

Ki turned to leave the coach. Before he could open the door he felt a hand land on his shoulder, a very heavy hand. He turned to find himself face to face, indeed almost nose to nose, with the bearded man.

"It is thanks I give to you," said the man in a booming voice. "You bring to me back my little Lena."

Ki's spirits fell. So the lovely Lena was married. He glanced at her, at her beautiful blue eyes that were like two small lakes, at her sleek hair that was bound in a coiled braid and fastened at the nape of her neck, at her voluptuous body. He almost sighed with regret.

"You're welcome," he said.

"Lena goes to do what we all must sometimes do," the man said, and Lena lowered her gaze and blushed. "My Lena did not know which way to come back here to me. She say the conductor be bad with her. Lena say he call her Bohunk."

Ki was about to ask the man what the name meant when Lena looked up, smiled, and said, "I thank you, sir, for saving me from trainmaster."

"You speak English!" Ki exclaimed in surprise.

"Some I speak, yes. A little. Trainmaster make it all go out of my head so I can speak only Serbian."

"We are Slavs," the man announced proudly. "All people here are Slavs." He waved one huge arm about to encompass the people in the crowded coach, most of whom were men as rough-hewn as he was himself.

"I was glad I could be of help," Ki said.

"This country, very strange. We not know always how things should be, what thing one must do. Lena has never been before on train."

"We are from Chicago," Lena told Ki shyly. "That is American city on big lake."

"Yes, I know. I've been there."

"We go to work in mines," the man announced. "Oh, my manners I forget. I am Josip Tito. This my daughter, Lena."

Ki's spirits not only revived but actually soared when he heard the words that told him Lena was not Josip's wife as he had at first incorrectly assumed.

"How do you do, Mr. Tito? Lena?"

"We do good when we get down in mine and dig up gold," Josip answered jovially. "Then we get ourselves rich."

One of the men in the mob behind Josip called out something in a foreign tongue.

Josip quickly responded in his resounding voice. Then, to Ki, he said, "Dmitri tell me we not get rich. I tell him maybe so not. But we not stay poor either, I tell him." Josip grinned, baring thick white teeth, and slapped Ki on the back, almost knocking him down.

"Papa work in mine in old country," Lena volunteered. "Papa strong man."

Ki, recovering from Papa's friendly slap on the back, could not argue the point.

"You are not of this land," Lena observed.

"I was born in Japan," Ki told her.

"You speak good the English."

"I have been here many years."

"Come, man of Japan," boomed Josip. "You will a drink have with me and these my friends."

Ki started to decline the invitation, but Josip wrapped an arm around his shoulders and led him into the midst of the mob of men, preventing him from doing so. A bottle was produced, its lower two-thirds bound in straw.

Josip took it from the man holding it and thrust it at Ki. "You drink."

Someone began to play an accordion. A woman began to sing a soft song that sounded like a gypsy lament.

Ki shook his head and tried to hand the bottle back to Josip. Josip declined it, repeating, "You drink."

An invitation? A command?

Ki uncorked the bottle, put it to his mouth, tipped his head backward, and took a sip of the bottle's contents.

He almost howled aloud as the liquor burned its way down into his belly. His eyes began to water. He coughed.

"Is good, yes?" Josip said. "Is Lithuanian drink. Stanislaus make it good." He pointed to a grinning man with a blond handlebar mustache who mimed drinking from the bottle, rolling his gray eyes as he did so.

"Again," Josip said to Ki. "First drink for good luck. Second drink, like Americans say, for fun."

This time Ki tilted the bottle but blocked its mouth with his tongue. As he lowered the bottle after appearing to have downed a deep draught, applause broke out in the coach.

It gave way to shouts and then to screams as the coach shook violently, as if it had just been seized by a giant hand, and then, with a resounding roar and the shrill sound of breaking glass, the entire train toppled off the tracks.

Chapter 3

The accordion music screeched its way into silence as Ki was thrown backward to fall against the side of the coach that had tilted at a forty-five degree angle. He grunted as his body struck a window and its glass smashed. He grunted again when someone fell on top of him, almost crushing his chest.

In the tangle of arms and legs around him, he could not at first make out who it was. Then, with the aid of sunlight reflecting off broken glass, he was able to discern the rough features of Josip Tito's face.

Josip rolled to one side and groaned, freeing Ki, who hastily scrambled to his feet among the people scattered about the coach, some of them unconscious, others too stunned to stir or even speak. He stood there a moment, unsteady on his feet and swaying slightly, but he managed to maintain his balance. He reached down and seized one of Josip's hands and helped the man to his feet.

"Lena" was all Josip could manage to mutter as he

scanned the coach in search of his daughter.

"Papa."

The call that was little more than a weak cry had come from the far end of the coach.

As both Josip and Ki fought their way through the coach's interior wreckage toward Lena, who was leaning at a precarious angle against a seat that had been ripped free of its floor bolts, the coach suddenly groaned mightily and then lurched downward.

Lena fell, disappearing from sight. Ki, as Josip stumbled and fell over a carpetbag jutting out from beneath the motionless body of a woman, reached Lena and helped her rise.

The pair stood there for a moment, neither of them speaking, Lena clinging to Ki so desperately that her fingernails cut through the fabric of his shirt and dug into the flesh of his arms.

All around them people were struggling to escape from the coach.

"Lena, are you all right?" Ki asked as her body trembled against his own.

"Not hurt bad. My leg—"

Ki looked down at the torn skirt of Lena's dress through which he could see the gash on her calf. It appeared to him to be a minor wound, although blood was seeping from it and staining her dress. "It's not deep," he told her. "You'll be fine."

"Papa?"

"Here, child," Josip answered as he joined Ki and Lena. "You are not hurt?"

"Not bad," Lena repeated. "You, Papa?"

"Apocalypse come, maybe it hurt Josip Tito. Not this little train smash."

Lena laughed and Ki thought he heard the first shrill notes of hysteria lurking in the sound. To stave it off, he began to guide Lena to the smashed door at one end of the coach. "Follow us, Josip!" he called over his shoulder as he was forced to elbow aside a man who tried frantically to pass him in his desperate hurry to escape from the wreckage.

The screaming had stopped. It had been replaced by moaning and groaning as injured passengers tried to make their way out of the coach by any means possible, including through the broken windows.

Ki reached the door of the coach with Lena leaning heavily against him and Josip following close behind. "Here we go," he said to Lena, easing her through the door. "Climb down to the ground. Here, I'll help you."

He helped Lena climb down and then he offered his hand to Josip.

"I can do for myself, but thank you much," Josip declared, and followed Lena down to the ground. Ki jumped down beside them and said, "I've got to go find a friend of mine."

Before either Lena or Josip could say anything to him, Ki went racing along the gravel roadbed that was almost totally obliterated by derailed coaches, unmindful of the shouting and the cursing and the violent fistfight that had broken out between two men for no reason that he could discern.

When he reached the coach he had been traveling in with Jessie, he saw no sign of her among the passengers outside it who were all standing dazed or talking in low tones among themselves. Without a moment's hesitation, he kicked in a window and then kicked the remaining fragments of glass from its frame. He bent down and thrust his head through the empty space he had made. He heard someone moaning inside the coach but could see no sign of Jessie. He eased his body into the coach and managed to stand up, his head pointing toward the windows above him on the opposite side of the coach.

"Jessie!"

No reply. He called her name again. At the same time he began to scramble over seats which were all tilted at odd angles toward the one in which Jessie and he had been sitting.

He found her sprawled on the floor in front of her seat, her body wedged between it and the seat in front that the crash had somehow shoved close together. She was lying on her back with her eyes closed.

A chill coursed through Ki at the sight of her lying there so still and pale. He forced himself to remain calm, part of his mind focusing once again on the *tai-ten* as he sought to link himself with the forces loose in the universe and to place himself in the center of their powerful flow.

He leaned over the seat in front of him and placed two fingers against the side of Jessie's neck. His face remained impassive when he felt a pulse pounding there, but inside his mind he was exulting at the discovery that Jessie had survived the crash. She was alive. He knew that. What he did not know and was almost afraid to find out was how badly she might be hurt.

The angry shouting and loud cursing he had heard earlier while on his way to Jessie continued outside the coach, but he paid no attention to it. He did pay attention to the problem facing him, which was how to get Jessie out from between the seats without aggravating any injuries she might have sustained or causing her any more.

He examined her body in relation to the two seats, the one on which she had been sitting and the one directly in front of her. He quickly saw that the front seat had been bent at a sharp angle, although the iron bolts that anchored it to the floor had remained in place. But, he saw with relief, not firmly in place. The bolts, all four of them, had been bent almost at right angles.

He bent down, oblivious of everything else now but his need to get Jessie out of the odd prison she was trapped in. He tried easing her slowly out from under the seat but found that he could move her no more than an inch before her body became lodged against one of the seat's armrests and would go no farther. He straightened and then tried to lift her, placing his hands under her armpits.

She moaned.

He stopped what he was doing, fearful of hurting her.

A puzzle, he thought. One as infuriating as any Zen koan. What is the sound of one hand clapping, he thought, recalling one of the koans that had always defeated him in his search for the answer to it. How to remove a beloved friend from danger without doing that friend further harm, he thought, making up his own koan on the spot.

His mind raced. He considered several possible methods and rejected them all. Then it came to him like a burst of bright light. Maybe he couldn't move *her* without running the risk of harming her, but he could move the *seat* that imprisoned her beneath it.

He maneuvered himself in such a way that he was able to exert force on the top of the backward-bent seat. He intended to try to bend the bolts that held the seat back toward their original positions so that the seat would once again be upright or reasonably so. He refused to acknowledge the fact that the strong iron bolts presented a formidable challenge to him insofar as each was more than a quarter of an inch in diameter. He took a deep breath, let it out, and put his shoulder to the task.

"Hey, you!"

Ki gave the man who had just appeared at the broken window above him with an iron crowbar in his hand only a brief glance as he continued to work at the task facing him.

42

"You a miner?" the man called down to him.

A second man appeared at the same broken window as Ki continued straining against the seat he was trying to force back into its original position.

"Come on, Max!" the second man yelled. "He's not one of them. The Bohunks were all in the last car. Let's go get us our share of 'em."

The two men disappeared.

Ki, as sweat broke out on his forehead, continued to work at the task he had set for himself. Below him, Jessie remained motionless, her breathing shallow.

The seat moved. Not much. Less than an inch. But that nearly unnoticeable distance buoyed Ki immeasurably. He redoubled his efforts. The seat moved—once again less than an inch. Then, an inch. The harsh sound of metal being tortured filled the empty car.

Ki braced his boots on the seat behind him and pushed with all his might, his eyes squeezed shut, sweat falling from his face in salty droplets.

Suddenly one of the bolts, with a terrible metallic squeal, shattered. Ki kept pushing. The second bolt on the same side shattered a moment later. As the left side of the seat, freed now from the floor, flew forward at a sharp angle, Ki almost lost his balance and fell upon Jessie. But he managed to hold on to the seat he had partially freed, his body a bridge suspended in the air above Jessie.

Moving carefully, he got one foot on the floor beneath him and then the other one. He let go of the seat and straightened up.

"Ki."

He had never been so glad to hear his name spoken by anyone in his entire life as he was to hear it spoken at that moment by Jessie. He knelt down beside her. "I'm here."

"What happened?"

"Are you all right?" he asked as he gently examined her

43

legs and arms for broken bones. To his immense relief, he found none.

"Groggy," Jessie whispered.

Ki helped her to sit up.

"I'm in one piece, at least," she said. "And I feel all right inside. But, oh, how my head hurts!"

Only then did Ki notice the large bump on her head, an injury that until now had been hidden from sight by her hair.

"I must have been knocked out."

"There's no doubt about that whatsoever. Do you think you can stand? We've got to get out of here. If you can't make it, I'll carry you."

"What a gallant offer." Jessie managed a smile. "The best I've had in days. But I'll turn it down—though it's greatly appreciated—in favor of trying to get my sea legs back."

Ki helped her to her feet and stood beside her while she got her bearings. Then he bent down and picked up her hat and handed it to her.

As she put it on, she winced.

"We can get out of here through that window," Ki said, pointing to the window he had broken to get into the coach. "Be careful. I tried to get rid of all the broken glass, but there might still be some left in the frame. We'll have to squeeze through."

"What's all that shouting about outside?" Jessie asked, frowning.

"I don't know. I suppose everybody's just excited as a result of what happened."

But both Ki and Jessie knew that his explanation could not have been correct when they emerged through the window—Ki first so he could help Jessie out—and found themselves facing a series of miniature brawls taking place on the roadbed and even on top of the train's overturned cars.

"What's going on?" Jessie asked as she stared incredulously at the scene before her which she thought resembled nothing so much as a mob of men gone mad.

Ki had no answer for her.

"You Bohunks have no right to take a man's livelihood away from him!" roared a battling man as he attacked one of the men who had been in the last car with Ki, Josip, and Lena.

The man could say no more because the taller man he was fighting planted a fist right between his eyes. The struck man staggered backward, stumbled over the exposed root of a tree growing at the edge of the roadbed, and fell to the ground.

He lay there in front of Jessie and Ki for a moment, shaking his head, and then he started to rise.

When he was back on his feet again, but before he could return to the fray, Ki grabbed him by the shoulder and asked, "What's going on here?"

The man drew back a fist, ready to lay Ki low, but Ki threw up his right forearm to block the blow. Twisting the man's arm behind his back and holding him in a way that kept him from moving without badly hurting himself, Ki said, "I asked you a question and I want an answer."

"You know what's going on same as I do!" the man shouted. "You foreigners have all come to take the food out of our mouths—and out of our families' mouths, too."

"I don't know what you're talking about."

"Let me loose and I'll kill you, you dirty strikebreaker!"

The man's last word caused Ki and Jessie to exchange glances.

"This man is no strikebreaker," Jessie said firmly. "He was traveling to Cripple Creek with me, but not to help break any strike."

45

"Well, those Bohunks from Chicago are strikebreakers sure enough. Some of the mine owners got together and had them shipped in. Well, us miners are here to keep them out of Cripple Creek."

"You miners derailed the train," Ki accused.

"Damn right we did. A few of us felled some trees and dragged them onto the tracks just out of sight around that curve back there so the train would ram them and go over."

"Who's leading you fellows?" Ki asked.

"Dan is, that's who."

"Dan Calhoun?" Jessie inquired.

"The same. That's him right over there. The man wearing the derby hat and the devilish grin. Now, let me loose!"

Ki released the man, who went running right into the middle of a fight between two men.

Jessie stared at Dan Calhoun as he swung a fist in what she recognized as a highly skilled fashion. The man he was fighting took a right jab and then a left hook. He retaliated with a savage blow to Calhoun's chin, which succeeded only in tilting Calhoun's derby to one side, where it sat at a rakish angle.

Calhoun was a tall man, topping six feet. His skin was smooth and pale, contrasting sharply with his curly black hair, which tumbled down over his coat collar and framed his square face like an ebony helmet. He had a broad forehead and an almost patrician nose. His full lips hinted at sensuality.

His eyes of amber made Jessie remember a prowling lion she had once seen in a zoo. He was, altogether, a striking figure of a man, she decided, and then winced as Calhoun drove his right fist into his opponent's face, mashing his lips into a bloody pulp and knocking two teeth out of the man's mouth. He followed up with a furious flurry of blows that put his opponent on the ground, from which he did not rise.

"Jessie, stay here," Ki said hurriedly. "I've got to go."

"Where?" Jessie asked too late.

Ki was gone.

He went sprinting to where he had seen Josip Tito being attacked by a trio of men, all of them smaller than Josip himself, but, in their combined strength, more than a match for the lone man.

Along the way he paused only long enough to pick up a lodgepole pine branch which he was pleased to see was not rotted. The limb measured just under six feet and Ki intended to use it as a reasonable facsimile of the martial arts *bo*, or straight staff, a highly effective weapon of self-defense which had originated centuries earlier in Okinawa, having evolved from the *tenbin*, a stick or bar borne across the shoulders from which buckets were suspended.

The *bo* was a tribute to oriental ingenuity and had developed in direct response to a repressive order of the Japanese government around the year 1314 A.D. which forbade the inhabitants of the island from owning any weapons. The people of Okinawa then turned not only to open-handed martial arts for protection but also to the use of their basic farm implements as weapons of which the *tenbin* was a classic example.

Josip was down on the ground when Ki reached him. One of his attackers was on top of him and pummeling him with both fists. The other two men stood on either side of Josip as he tried to fight off the man straddling him.

Ki took up a position just behind Josip's head. Wasting no time, he proceeded to practice the art of *bojutsu* in which he had been well-trained. Gripping his *bo* in both hands, he first executed a *yoko-uchi*, a side strike, to the left side of the head of the man on top of Josip. He followed immediately with a *gyaku-yoko-uchi*, a reverse side strike, to the right side of the man's head.

The combined blows, following hard and fast upon one

47

another, knocked the man out. He fell heavily to the ground.

His two companions, after recovering from the shock induced in them by Ki's sudden appearance and his unorthodox means of doing battle, let out simultaneous roars of outrage and lunged at him.

He held his ground, twirling the tree limb that served him as a *bo* above his head and delivering a side strike to the man on his right. He immediately reversed the maneuver and downed the second man coming at him. He was about to deliver a follow-up strike after his *ichimonjimawashi* movements, but before he could do so, Lena appeared out of nowhere and leaped upon the back of the first man Ki had struck, who was down on his hands and knees, his head hanging low.

She pounded both of her fists on the man's already dazed head, her jaw set, her eyes wild with fury. The man let out a startled yelp as he tried desperately to protect his head from her blows. He failed to do so. Lena continued to batter him mercilessly, firmly gripping his body between her knees so that he couldn't dislodge her from her attack position.

When his companion, who had also fallen under Ki's onslaught, made a grab for Lena, Josip sprang to his feet and seized the man with both hands. He lifted him off the ground, held him high above his head as he turned in a circle, and then threw him against the trunk of a nearby tree.

When the man lay motionless on the ground, Josip turned his attention to the man Ki had knocked senseless, who was now rising, his fists tightly clenched at his sides. One blow from Josip's right hand broke the man's nose. It also broke his nerve. Covering his bleeding nose with both hands, he turned and fled.

His companion finally managed to dislodge Lena. Then he, too, fled.

"Is good job you do with stick," Josip told Ki. "You bust men's brains."

"You two didn't need my help," Ki said modestly. "Between the pair of you, you could have taken on this whole bunch without help from anyone."

Lena joined her father, who put an arm around her. Both of them were breathless but smiling.

"They say to me I be strikebreaker," Josip remarked after a moment and with a frown. "What is it, 'strikebreaker'?"

Ki explained. "It's a term used for a man who will come to a place where workers are on strike—"

"On strike?" Lena interjected, obviously puzzled.

Ki explained the meaning of the word *strike*. "A strikebreaker is a man who will work when and where other men won't. The other men go on strike—understand?" When his two listeners nodded, he continued, "You are a strikebreaker, Mr. Tito, because you're going to work in a gold mine in Cripple Creek, which means you will be taking the job of a miner who has gone on strike for better pay and better working conditions."

"No one tell any of this to us in Chicago," Josip said slowly. "Men come. They say to us they come from gold mines. They say to us they need miners. I take job from them. My friends take jobs from them. No one tell us of strike. No one say we be strikebreakers if we come to Cripple Creek."

"Well, that's the way the land lies, it seems," Ki said solemnly. "I didn't know what was going on until all this." He gestured at the fighting that was still going on in the area, his gesture encompassing the damaged train as well.

At that moment one of the strikers jumped Josip from

behind. Josip shook himself like a dog emerging from a pond, and the man fell to the ground.

"Take my Lena!" he yelled to Ki. "Someplace safe you take her. Give me!"

Josip ripped the makeshift *bo* from Ki's hand and began to flail about with it, bowling over men in every direction who had been attacking the men he had been traveling with.

"Come on!" Ki said, seizing Lena's hand.

She tried to break free of him. "I go fight, too," she insisted.

"No, you won't go fight, too," he told her, and proceeded to drag her, protesting all the way, into the shelter and comparative safety of the trees lining the tracks.

Everywhere Jessie looked, as she stood beside the wrecked train, she saw women with folded triangular kerchiefs over their heads and tied beneath their chins, shawls over their shoulders, many of them with small children in their arms or standing terrified and silent by their sides. Some of them were weeping openly. Others stood with stony faces like the faces of the suffering everywhere who have learned a bitter lesson and know that there is nothing they can do but endure.

Her gaze shifted to Dan Calhoun in the distance. He was shouting at the top of his voice but still not all of his words were audible to Jessie above the din the fighting men were making. She watched him collar a man and point him in the direction of a man fleeing toward the woods. She watched him punch the face of another man who came at him with a railroad tie he had evidently ripped free of the roadbed.

She could stand it no longer. She went stalking toward Calhoun, fire in her eyes, the heat of her anger bringing a flush to her face. When she reached him, she stepped directly in front of him, preventing him from seizing a man in a torn coat who had blood and bruises on his face.

"Just what do you think you're doing?" she shouted at him, planting her legs wide apart and her hands upon her hips.

Calhoun stared steadily at her. Then his eyes shifted from her face and began to roam up and down her body.

To Jessie's consternation, he tipped his hat and bowed to her.

"You could have killed people by blocking the tracks with those trees," she accused.

"I had nothing to do with that. When I got here, some of the men had already felled trees and hauled them onto the tracks. We'd planned to block the train with our bodies, not with trees, but a few hotheads got here first—and got out of line, it would seem."

"A few hotheads indeed! It seems to me that you're one of them with your wild rhetoric that was reported in the newspaper and your—"

Calhoun interrupted her by asking, "To what do I owe this visit, Miss—"

"Jessica Starbuck. You owe this visit to your dangerous ringmastering of this equally dangerous circus."

"Jessica Starbuck," Calhoun repeated, his face darkening. "Miss Mighty Millions," he sneered. "Come to see the animals perform, have you, Miss Starbuck, to carry your circus analogy one step further?"

"It would most certainly seem so," Jessie shot back. "You and these other animals are putting on what I consider to be a most shameful performance."

"It is not shameful for men to fight for their rights against those who would abuse and, indeed, unlife them if it should come down to that."

"I haven't the slightest idea of what you're talking about."

"I am talking about these strikebreakers," Calhoun bellowed, pointing at them as they continued to do bloody battle with the strikers. "They have been brought here by the mine owners—by you, Miss Starbuck, and the other killer capitalists who own and operate gold mines in Cripple Creek. They have been brought here to take our places in your mines. They have been hired to break our strike and—"

"One moment, if you please, Mr. Calhoun!"

Calhoun, his mouth open, said nothing.

"I had no direct hand in bringing these men here to break your strike or for any other reason. I know nothing about them—how they got here or who brought them here. I hasten to add that I strongly resent your accusation—your *unfounded* accusation. You called me a killer capitalist. Well, although it is unladylike and beneath my dignity, I call you, Mr. Calhoun, nothing more than a common hoodlum."

"You know my name."

"I also know that your attempts to intimidate these men you call strikebreakers will not work. Nor will I be intimidated by your vicious brawling, Mr. Calhoun. I have dealt with rowdies like you before. Successfully, I might add."

"Now I'm a rowdy! Is that a step up or a step down from common hoodlum?"

Jessie ignored the question. "Understand one thing, Mr. Calhoun. You will not stop me from operating the Empire Mine. I will do whatever I have to do to keep it open. Your strike will not stop me from doing that, I promise you. I told you that I had nothing to do with bringing the men your men are attacking to Cripple Creek. But I tell you now, and I trust you are listening to me for your own good, that I will hire a hundred strikebreakers—a thousand, if necessary—to see to it that you do not interfere with the profitable operation of the Empire."

"Don't you get in my way, Miss Starbuck," Calhoun muttered between gritted teeth. "You say you've dealt with men like me before. Well and good. I would like you to know that I have dealt with women like you before and not one of the little baggages has meant so much as this to me!" Calhoun snapped his fingers in front of Jessie's face.

Her anger, no longer under control, erupted. Almost before she knew what she was doing, she had slapped Calhoun's face.

Damn you, Dan Calhoun, she thought, as Josip Tito and his friends finally succeeded in driving off Calhoun and his strikers.

Ki led Lena deeper into the woods. Her hand in his felt cold, and as he glanced at her, he could see the tension in her face and body and he could sense the fear she still felt.

They moved through a dappled glade and then across a patch of mossy ground that was bordered by wild flowers. Minutes later they came to a creek where the only sound in the forest was its bubbling over the rocks in its path.

"Let's sit down here," Ki suggested.

Lena looked back over her shoulder.

He squeezed her hand reassuringly. "We're safe here."

Lena sat down, her legs on one side, her hands clenched in her lap.

Ki reached out and undid them. "Relax," he whispered, holding both of her hands in his. "There's nothing to be afraid of here."

"But Papa—back there—"

"Your papa can take care of himself, I'm pretty sure about that."

Lena nervously gnawed at her lower lip.

A crow suddenly cawed overhead, the sound shattering the stillness of the forest and causing Lena to throw her arms around Ki for protection.

"It's all right," he assured her, welcoming the warmth of her body against his own.

She snuggled against Ki, her cheek resting against his chest. Then, lifting her head, she gazed into his eyes.

He thought he could read the message of desire he saw in them. He bent and kissed her lightly on the lips.

She didn't react at first, but then, as their kiss continued, she began to respond until she was fiercely matching Ki's growing passion.

His hands found her breasts and fondled them. She responded to his caresses by reaching behind her and beginning to unbutton her dress.

Their lips parted.

Lena sprang to her feet and began to undress. Ki did the same. Then, as Lena lay back down on the thick grass growing beside the creek, he sank down upon her with a sigh and an exhalation of breath that was hot upon her cheek.

He adroitly adjusted his body to cover hers. He nudged her legs farther apart with his own. Then he was fingering her, but he quickly found out that such ministrations were unnecessary. She was not only moist; her juices drowned his probing finger.

Fully aroused now, his erection throbbed and spasmed as it worked its way into her. He raised his upper body, supporting himself on his hands, so that he could look down at Lena as he began to move with tantalizing slowness within her.

He watched her eyes take on that glow that desire always kindles in passionate women. He stoked that fire with his iron-hard shaft that was buried deep inside the woman under him, who twisted from side to side while simultaneously thrusting her pelvis up to draw him even more deeply into her body as she sought his satisfaction along with her own.

"Is it—" he began.

"Good," she murmured between barely parted lips as her hands rose and clasped his shoulders. "So good. So *wonderful*."

She groaned then as he inadvertently, in his enthusiastic thrusting, slipped out of her. She seized his shaft and placed it within her again. Her body closed upon it, massaged it.

Ki threw back his head, his eyes closed now, his lips parted. He could feel the mounting tension that proceded the thrilling climax he knew was coming, was now only moments away. He shifted position slightly—drawing out the pleasure that was a kind of exquisite agony—and then he exploded. He cried out, a kind of animalistic howl. He dropped back down upon Lena. His hands went under her buttocks. He lifted her up toward him and held her there as he continued to shoot a steady stream of his seed into her.

Lena cried out as she, too, climaxed.

Ki drew a deep breath and buried his face in her neck, becoming aware of the sweet clean smell of her blond hair. He kissed her ear, raised his head slightly and kissed her chin. Then her nose and lips.

She eased down on the grass until she was able to touch his nipples with her hot lips. She went from one to the other and back again—tasting, biting, teasing.

Ki responded. He held Lena close, unmindful of her fingernails that were raking his back and buttocks, the slight pain adding spice to their second coupling.

This time Lena climaxed first, but she continued to match Ki's wild rhythm until he ejaculated. Only then did she release her hold on him. Only then did a drained but satisfied Ki withdraw from her and flop down on the ground by her side.

He fondled her breasts, tweaking her erect nipples between his fingertips.

Lena stroked his still-stiff shaft. Lightly at first and then more vigorously.

Ki was about to tell her that it was no use, that he was empty. But she proved him wrong. Not once but twice over the next uncounted number of delightful minutes.

Later, as they both lay quietly on the grass together, Lena spoke. "We go back now?"

Ki sat up. "Yes, we'll go back now."

They got up and dressed and then made their way back the way they had come, Ki once again leading Lena by the hand. When they neared the site of the train wreck, he told her to wait where she was while he went ahead to scout the scene.

He returned for her minutes later. "It's over. Your papa's fine. I'll take you to him."

★

Chapter 4

"The man is intolerable!" Jessie exclaimed late that night as she finished unpacking her clothes, cartridge belt, and .38 caliber Colt revolver in the room she had rented in the Nugget Hotel in Cripple Creek.

"So was the ride here in those wagons the railroad sent to fetch us," Ki remarked as he sat in a chair near the window, his own unpacking completed earlier in his room next door.

"You're not taking me seriously," Jessie protested, giving him an annoyed glance.

"It's true. I was so bounced around in the wagon I rode in that my teeth practically fell out. But I guess we have to thank the railroad for sending wagons for us. If they hadn't, we'd have had a long hot walk back to town."

"Well, we survived that ride, uncomfortable as it was. But I'm not sure I, for one, am going to survive Dan Calhoun."

"From what I saw of him, he seems a presentable

enough fellow. Why do you say he's intolerable?"

"Ah-ha! So you were listening to me after all."

Ki smiled.

"Ki, it's his personality. His attitude. Oh, I suppose some women might find him attractive enough."

"Some women," Ki repeated.

"But *this* woman finds him irritating, obnoxious, and—and—"

"How about thoroughly objectionable?"

"Stop teasing me."

"Well, I have to admit that Calhoun harmed a lot of people by blocking the tracks the way he did."

"He claims he had nothing to do with that. He told me his plan was to block the tracks by having his men stand on them, but by the time he got there, some of the strikers had felled trees and dragged them onto the tracks."

"Now you're defending him."

"I am not! I'm just telling you what he told me."

Ki burst out laughing.

"You are just about as intolerable as Dan Calhoun," Jessie declared hotly. But then she, too, began to smile and then to laugh. "What happened to make you run off so suddenly during the brawl outside of town?"

"I saw a man who seemed to be in trouble. He was a man I'd met when I escorted the woman—her name was Lena Tito by the way—back to her coach on the train. In fact, the man was her father, Josip."

"Don't let our friend, Dan Calhoun, know you've been consorting with strikebreakers. He might not like it."

"That brings something to mind," Ki said thoughtfully.

"What is it?"

"Mr. Tito claims that he and the men with him didn't know that they were hired to come here to help break the strike. He told me they had merely been offered mining jobs. He said he didn't know they would be taking jobs

58

away from other miners. I was wondering if your mine manager at the Empire might have had a hand in hiring some of those Chicago-based men in what has got to be called a pretty slick move."

Jessie shook her head. "I don't think Fred Bolan would have taken part in such a deal. Fred's a forthright and honest man. He's the kind who calls a spade a spade. If he had hired any of those men to replace the strikers, he would have told them exactly what the situation here was and what they were getting themselves into."

"You're sure of that?"

"Reasonably sure, yes. Not positive, of course. I intend to discuss the matter with him."

"If Mr. Tito told me the truth, and I have no reason to believe he lied to me, then he and the other men on the train are as much victims in this matter as are the miners who've gone out on strike."

"There are other victims, too. Namely, the mine owners."

"It's a bad situation no matter from which point of view you look at it. It looks to me like it's one that can only get worse before it gets better. Maybe a whole lot worse."

Early the next morning, after a breakfast of ham and scrambled eggs in a restaurant across the street from the Nugget Hotel, Jessie and Ki rented a carriage at the local livery barn and drove out to Starbuck Enterprises' Empire Gold Mine.

Jessie stopped the rig in front of the small shed which served as the mine's business office. She braked the carriage, wrapped her reins around the brake handle, and stepped down from the carriage to join Ki in front of the shed's door on which she knocked.

"Come in."

In response to the male voice she had recognized as

Fred Bolan's, Jessie opened the wooden door and stepped into the office where Bolan, his left arm in a sling, sat behind his desk.

"Jessie!" he cried when he saw her. "Well, aren't you a sight for sore eyes now!" he added, getting up and rounding his desk to pump Jessie's outstretched hand.

Bolan was a short man with a paunch that drooped below his belt. His hair was not only thinning but graying. His cheeks were plump pouches and his jowls were heavy. His blue eyes twinkled.

"Fred, I read about the shooting in the newspaper in Denver. How is your arm coming along?"

"It's fine, thanks. Looks a lot worse than it really is."

"But the newspaper said the shot had broken bones in your arm."

"One thing you've got to remember about newspapers, Jessie, is this. Paper won't refuse ink. The writer of that article exaggerated the seriousness of my wound. Sure, some bone was chipped but not really broken. I'll be out of this sling in a day or two and back in business as usual."

"I'm relieved to hear that. The newspaper said you didn't know who had shot you."

"That's right. I don't know who it was. All I know for sure was that I was shot from behind. The round went in the back of my arm and out the front."

"You may not know the name of the man who shot you," Jessie said, "but you must know he was a coward to do a thing like that."

"Backshooters always are cowards," Bolan agreed, and then, "I got your telegraph message. I was glad to hear you were coming to pay us a visit."

"I made up my mind to do so after I received your last report which mentioned the possibility of labor trouble. I decided it might prove to be worth my while to make a trip here to see how things were for myself."

"I'm glad you did that, Jessie." Bolan ran a hand through what was left of his hair and sadly shook his head. "We have more trouble here now than does a steer at heel fly time, and that's a sorry fact but one I must tell you."

"I know about the strike. I—oh, before I forget—let me introduce you to my good friend, Ki."

"It's pleased I am to make your acquaintance, sir," Bolan declared, vigorously pumping Ki's hand.

Jessie continued, "I also know that men have been hired in Chicago and brought here to work in the mines. Ki met one of them, as a matter of fact. Are you using any of those men in the Empire, Fred?"

Bolan's eyes shifted away from Jessie. "Yes, I am. I hired a number of them last night. I didn't think you'd want the mine to lie idle while the miners are on strike."

"I'm certainly not keen on seeing the mine shut down. On the other hand, I must confess to you that I'm not entirely comfortable with the prospect of employing strike-breakers."

"Neither am I, Jessie, to tell the whole truth," Bolan admitted somewhat sheepishly. "These days it often does seem to me that a man must more and more often choose, not the unadulterated good, but between the lesser of two evils."

"Never an easy choice," Ki commented.

"That, too, is a sad fact," Bolan said sorrowfully. "If things keep up like this, Jessie, I shall lose the rest of my hair before too long as a direct result of all the worrying I've been doing of late."

"What are you paying the men you've just hired?" Jessie inquired.

"Two-fifty a day."

"*Two*-fifty per day?" Jessie's eyes narrowed. "The last I heard the prevailing wage was three-fifty per day."

"True enough, it was."

61

"Then I don't understand the reason for the lower wage scale. Lower, in fact, by one-third."

"It wasn't my doing," Bolan said after a moment.

"Not your doing? You're the Empire's manager. If setting the wage scale isn't up to you, then who does determine it?"

"I determine it," Bolan said, obviously uncomfortable with Jessie's probing. "But let's say that I have had rather compelling advice in the matter. Advice freely given by Mr. Horace Willoughby."

"Horace Willoughby," Jessie repeated. "The owner of the Bluebell Mine."

"He's also the owner of many other claims in the area, is Mr. Horace Willoughby. He's been expanding his holdings at a right smart clip of late. He is the gentleman who has taken it upon himself to make it known to those of us in Cripple Creek who are responsible for hiring and paying miners that, in light of the strike and in a concerted effort to break the will of the strikers, we should all pay the new men *less* than we formerly paid our regular employees."

"To teach those rebellious employees a lesson," Ki suggested.

Bolan nodded, still not looking directly at Jessie. " 'Tis a bitter lesson that's being taught, let me tell you both. It has been difficult for many men with families to make ends meet on three-fifty a day, let alone the almost paltry sum of two-fifty, which is the one at which Willoughby says he expects to hire back his miners once this unpleasantness— that's what he calls the strike—'this unpleasantness'—is over."

"You agreed with his position, Fred?" Jessie asked.

"I did. But reluctantly. And I did to preserve that united front that Willoughby's so keen on and which he claims is our best weapon against the strikers."

"Why didn't you let me know about this wage decision?"

"I learned about it myself only two days ago when Willoughby came by here. There wasn't time to notify you. Then, too, I felt I should be the one to make the decision as manager of the mine. To tell you the truth, Jessie, I think the decision was a good one in a business sense if not altogether in a humanitarian sense. I say this because I tend to agree on one point with Willoughby and that point is that the mine owners should indeed present a united front in the face of—"

"This unpleasantness," Jessie said rather harshly.

"This Mr. Willoughby may very well have a point, Jessie," Ki remarked.

"Perhaps so." Jessie was silent for a moment. Then, "I'd like to see what conditions are like down in the mine, Fred. If you're busy, Ki and I can go down there by ourselves."

"I'll go with you," Bolan volunteered, and led the way out of the shed and through a door into a nearby and immense building that housed the mine's hoisting works.

Ki stared in astonishment at the building's forty-foot ceiling and then at the several large square openings in the wooden floor from which gushed great clouds of steam.

Bolan led the way to one of the cages which was suspended above one of the openings in the floor.

Ki, following behind him and Jessie, stared up at the huge wooden spools which, he estimated, were at least fifteen feet in diameter and around which were wound three-quarter-inch-thick cables of tightly braided wire.

Bolan, noticing her interest in the spools, commented, "That's the way we lower the miners into the shaft and haul them and the ore up."

"You're telling me the cages go down into that steam?" Ki asked uneasily.

"They do," Bolan replied.

"But that's live steam."

"The men get used to it," Bolan told him. "This way." He ushered first Jessie and then Ki into the cage.

They were no sooner inside it than Bolan gave a signal to one of the engineers manning the nearest of the hoisting engines.

It roared into life, adding its loud metallic voice to the din arising from the machinist's, carpenter's, and blacksmith's shops located inside the building.

Ki caught a brief glimpse of the braided wire on one of the huge spools as it began to unwind before the cage containing him, Jessie, and Bolan began to descend at a dizzying speed through the hot moist steam into a limbo of candles flickering in the blackness, a limbo in which the half-heard shouts of men echoed in languages other than English, a limbo in which huge timbers flashed upward past the descending cage and then were gone, while the sound of countless picks striking rock threatened to split his eardrums.

The shaft seemed to Ki to fly upward at an incredible speed. He gripped one of the iron uprights of the cage to help keep his balance and avoid falling from it.

"Don't do that!" Jessie told him, pulling his hand away from the upright. "Stand as close to the center of the cage as you can or you might have a hand or a foot torn off."

Ki accepted her warning in silence, releasing his hold on the upright and moving closer to the center of the cage through which steam was billowing up from below. He began to sweat as a result of the intense heat.

The cage suddenly lurched to a halt. The squealing of the unwinding wire stopped.

"This way," Bolan said, stepping out of the cage. "Let's follow the main drift over there. It runs north-south along the line of the lode."

Ki had to bend over slightly as they walked to avoid striking his head on the rocky outcroppings in the uneven ceiling.

"I see we have a few more crosscuts than I recall from when I visited here last year," Jessie observed.

"Nine altogether," said Bolan with a trace of pride.

"What's that?" Ki inquired, pointing to a vertical shaft.

"It's called a winze," Jessie answered. "Those short shafts run up and down to connect with other levels of the mine. Mind your step here, Ki. Don't stumble over those tracks."

Ki cautiously avoided the narrow-gauge ore-cart tracks.

They moved on in the candle-lit crosscuts, the hot air they breathed full of dust. A candle fell from a rocky ledge. Bolan stamped it out.

"This strikes me as a pretty dangerous place," Ki commented.

"The world itself is a dangerous place," Bolan stated offhandedly. "We all take risks as we make our wary way through it, willingly or not. A mine isn't much different from the rest of the world."

Ki succumbed to a fit of coughing as a result of the ubiquitous dust floating in the air.

"Step lively!" Bolan warned.

Ki and Jessie quickly stepped to one side as mules pulled and men pushed ore carts past them toward the cages which would hoist them to the surface. All around them, men were working with picks and sledges and drills, some of them bare-chested, all of them drenched with sweat.

"It certainly is hot down here," Ki commented, wiping his face with a handkerchief.

"It is that," Bolan agreed.

"The heat," Jessie said, "comes from subterranean fires

burning below the lode. Where is the ice chamber located, Fred?"

"This way."

Ki and Jessie followed the mine manager as he made his way to the left, and moments later the trio came to a lamp-lit and stoutly timbered chamber just off the main drift.

As Ki entered it, he let out a sigh of relief as cool air swept over him.

"You can get a drink of cold water from one of those barrels," Jessie told him. "In those other barrels over there, there's ice."

She went to one of the latter and withdrew a small chunk of ice which she used to rub across her forehead and cheeks.

Ki used a tin cup to drink from one of the barrels, filling it twice before his thirst was finally satisfied.

The sound of men's voices drifted toward them. Then several men entered the ice chamber, Josip Tito among them, all of them obviously surprised to see a woman in their midst.

"Mr. Tito," Ki said in greeting. "It's good to see you again. I'd like you to meet a friend of mine, Miss Jessica Starbuck. She is the owner of this mine. Jessie, this is the man I told you I met on the train, Josip Tito."

Josip smiled and bowed to Jessie. He showed her his hands, which were dirty, to wordlessly explain why he did not offer to shake hands with her.

"I'm pleased to meet you, Mr. Tito," she said.

"You work in mine, too?" Josip asked Ki.

"No, I'm on—I guess you could call it an inspection tour."

"Nice mine," Josip said, dipping a cup full of ice water and downing it. "Water we have here. Ice we have, also. Not like in old country. No water in mines there. No ice. You make good job for us, Miss Starbuck."

"Mr. Bolan and I have always tried to provide our men with the best possible working conditions, Mr. Tito."

"Yes, you do that thing. Give good wage, too."

Jessie exchanged glances with Bolan, but she said nothing.

"Seen enough?" Bolan asked her. "Ready to go back up?"

"Yes."

As Jessie was about to leave the ice chamber, Josip bowed her out.

The trio made their way back the way they had come, passing miners along the way who were attacking the veins of ore with picks. As they approached a pair of miners who were working as a team using a drill and sledge, Bolan suddenly put out his arm to prevent Ki and Jessie from advancing any farther. He did so just in time. As the sledge slammed heavily down on the drill, a huge chunk of ore fell away and immediately afterward a stream of steaming water gushed out of the outcropping.

"I saw a seeping," Bolan said. "Figured there was hot water back in there."

"What in the world's that?" Ki asked, as the flow of water slowed to a trickle. He pointed to the thick mass of what looked very much like precious stones glistening in the light of the candles which had just been revealed by the team of two miners.

"Iron and copper pyrites," Jessie told him as he continued staring at the crystal formation which glowed with a colorful fire.

"Pretty stuff," he remarked as they moved on into a square set of short timbers which were neatly joined into a boxlike frame.

They had no sooner done so than a candle guttered, flared into bright yellow life for an instant, and then went out, leaving them in near total darkness.

Several pairs of eyes gleamed in the faint glow from a more distant candle that was perched on a rocky ledge just beyond the square set.

"Rats," Jessie said, grimacing.

They carefully avoided the rodents as they made their way back to the cage, where Bolan pulled on a rope which caused a hammer to strike a bell next to the engineer's station in the hoisting works above, giving the man the signal that the cage was ready to be raised.

Within minutes they were stepping out of the cage onto the noisy floor of the hoisting works.

"I don't see how they do it," Ki said, wiping his sweaty forehead. "That's one tough way to make a living. Mining gold, I mean."

"It takes strong—and brave—men to work the mines," Jessie commented.

"They deserve every cent they earn down there," Ki said.

His statement caused Jessie to turn pensive as she thought that he was right and that the men in the mine below did indeed deserve all that they earned while working under such difficult and potentially hazardous conditions. It occurred to her that she was thinking in a way that would almost surely match the thoughts of Dan Calhoun. She found that insight both interesting and unsettling.

"Mr. Bolan!" shouted the engineer who had hoisted them to the surface, his hands cupped around his mouth to make himself heard above the noise in the building. "Mr. Willoughby's outside waiting to have a word with you."

Bolan gave the man an acknowledging wave and then led the way out of the hoisting works.

As Jessie emerged blinking into the bright sunlight, she shielded her eyes from the sun with one hand. She was able to make out a wagon standing not far away in which were seated two men, a driver and a passenger. She recognized the latter as Horace Willoughby.

Willoughby was a corpulent man whose clothes were too tight for him. His excess flesh seemed to be doing constant battle with them as if trying to escape their confines. His lips were thick and his chin sank into folds of flesh that hid his neck. His closely set eyes were gray and had a tendency to dart here and there as if in constant search of something.

"Good day to you, Mr. Willoughby," Bolan called out as he made his way over to the carriage. "How are you, Buster?"

The driver Bolan had just addressed merely shrugged. He seemed far more interested in Jessie than in answering Bolan's question. His pink tongue slid between his lips to lick them as he continued staring at Jessie, the reins of his rig wrapped around his fisted hands. His cheeks and chin were stubbled with several days' growth of wiry black beard. His complexion was sallow, as if it were a stranger to the sun. His brown eyes never seemed to blink.

"What is this, Fred?" Willoughby asked with a flourish in Jessie's direction. "Here I come calling on you on a matter of business and I find you entertaining a lovely lady."

"You know Miss Starbuck, I believe."

"I do."

Bolan turned and beckoned to Jessie and Ki. When they had joined him beside the carriage, he said, "I understand you know Mr. Willoughby, Jessie. Mr. Willoughby, may I introduce Miss Starbuck's friend, Ki."

Greetings were exchanged then, after which Willoughby asked, "What brings you to our fair city, Miss Starbuck?"

"Business," Jessie answered rather curtly, wondering why she had taken an almost instant dislike to Willoughby. He was being pleasant, even charming, she silently chided herself. She was being irrational, she decided. She gave him a smile.

"The strike?"

Jessie nodded.

"Unpleasant business. It's what I came here to talk to your manager about. But, before we fellows get down to business, I wonder if I might invite you, Miss Starbuck—and your friend, Ki—to have supper at my home. As mine owners we have a great deal in common and thus a great deal to discuss. We have our professional futures to plan and our responses to the strikers to decide upon. My sister, Matilda, and I would be honored to have you in our home."

"It's very kind of you to invite us, Mr. Willoughby," Jessie said, forcing herself to sound pleased. With a glance at Ki, she added, "We would be pleased to have supper at your home."

"Splendid. Tonight?"

Jessie hesitated a moment and then, smiling again, said, "Tonight would be fine."

"Matilda and I shall expect you at seven o'clock, then."

Jessie turned and, with Ki at her side, made her way back to the carriage she had rented.

They were driving away from the mine when Ki said, "I got the distinct impression back there that you weren't exactly thrilled at Willoughby's invitation."

"The man makes me uncomfortable. Did you notice the way he smiled? I mean his mouth smiled. *He* didn't."

Just before seven o'clock that evening, Ki and Jessie drove up the drive to Horace Willoughby's home.

"Do my eyes deceive me?" Ki declared as they drove past a three-tiered fountain rising from the center of an ornamental pool set in the lawn.

"Peacocks," Jessie breathed as she stared at the two

70

fan-tailed male birds strutting across the lush green lawn.

"Are you up on your croquet?" Ki inquired, pointing to the hoops dotting the lawn and to the racks containing brightly painted wooden croquet balls and mallets.

He parked the carriage in front of the house, which was a three-storied structure with a wide veranda graced by tall white Doric columns. It was topped by a dome containing multicolored stained glass in its many windows.

Leaving the carriage, Ki and Jessie stepped up onto the veranda, which was crowded with wicker furniture. Using the ornate brass knocker, Ki knocked on the door.

It was promptly opened by a maid wearing a black floor-length dress, a white apron, and a pert white cap.

"The Willoughbys are expecting us," Jessie told her.

"One moment please."

The door shut.

It opened again minutes later, and the maid showed Jessie and Ki into a sitting room that was full of heavy rosewood furniture among which several potted palms sprouted in brass containers.

"Please be seated," the maid said. "Mr. Willoughby will be with you presently."

And he was. Horace Willoughby, smoking a cigar, came bustling into the sitting room several minutes later amid a cloud of gray smoke.

"How good of you both to come!" he boomed, shaking Ki's hand and kissing Jessie's. "Supper will be served shortly. Matilda will soon be joining us. I did mention my sister, Matilda, to you, did I not?"

"How about a before-supper drink? Whiskey, Ki? Sherry, Miss Starbuck?"

Without waiting for their assent, Willoughby poured the drinks, then handed a crystal goblet of sherry to Jessie and a cut-glass tumbler of Scotch whiskey to Ki. Then, after pouring whiskey into another tumbler for himself, he turned to his guests, raised his glass and proposed a toast.

"To the stamping out of the miners' strike."

Jessie's glass halted halfway to her lips. She watched Willoughby as he drank and then smacked his lips. What *was* it about the man that made her feel so hostile toward him? All he had done was propose a toast. . . .

An image of Josip Tito and the other men whom Bolan had hired appeared in her mind. A fragment of her brief conversation with Tito during their meeting down in the Empire Mine echoed now in her mind.

"Nice mine," she heard Josip say again. *"You make good job for us, Miss Starbuck."*

She lowered her glass, her sherry untasted.

"Ah, here she is," Willoughby announced. "My sister, Matilda."

A tall and slender woman stood in the archway leading to the sitting room. A woman with inky eyes which gazed uneasily on the three people in the room as she twisted a lace-trimmed handkerchief in her slightly trembling hands. Her sleek black hair was worn in a tightly coiled bun at the nape of her neck. Her severe black dress bared no inch of her flesh except for her hands and face.

Ki, watching her, thought of blond, blue-eyed Lena. Matilda was black—black eyes, black hair, black clothes. Lena was noon. Matilda was midnight. This Willoughby woman, he found himself thinking, could be attractive, maybe even pretty, if she'd just let herself relax. She looks like a fox that's heard the sound of the hunter's horn.

"Matilda," Willoughby said, "may I present Miss Jessica Starbuck and her friend, Ki."

"How nice to meet you both," Matilda said in a small voice. "Brother told me you would be joining us for supper. I do hope you'll find everything satisfactory."

"You have a perfectly lovely home, Miss Willoughby,"

Jessie said, thinking that Matilda sounded as if she were apologizing for something.

"It was all Brother's doing actually," Matilda declared, twisting her handkerchief. "He built this place and was good enough to ask me to keep house for him."

"You don't want anything to drink, do you, Matilda?" Willoughby asked. Before she could respond, he continued, "Then we'll go in to supper, shall we?"

They left their glasses—Willoughby's empty, Jessie's and Ki's untouched—behind them in the sitting room and made their way into a sumptuously furnished dining room.

Tapestries of hunting scenes hung on two of the four walls. Red velvet draperies adorned the windows. A silver service sat on a buffet table. A breakfront of polished wood contained an assortment of china and silver utensils. On the floor was an immense oriental rug.

The table was aglow with silver candelabra, each of which held more than twenty candles. Their light glistened on the champagne cooler which sat at the head of the table, the bottle in it poking its corked head out of glittering ice. Next to it was a silver cigar stand. The china was exquisite, almost translucent, with ropes of painted roses adorning the pieces beneath a flawless glaze.

Jessie suddenly became aware of the fact that Willoughby was behind her. She allowed him to seat her, noticing that he ignored his sister, who stood meekly waiting on the opposite side of the table. She was relieved when Ki took it upon himself to seat their hostess.

Servants appeared and the supper was served. There was a spicy onion soup followed by poached salmon. The main course was a crown roast of pork, flavored with garlic, and garnished with juicy slices of baked apples.

Throughout the meal Willoughby talked. He talked of his wide-ranging business interests which, he said with a laugh, just might one day match or even exceed Jessie's own. He talked of the "nuisance" the miners' strike had turned out to be. He talked of his possessions—their costs, their provenance. The tapestries, it turned out, had been purchased at auction in London "for absolutely outrageous prices" and had once been owned by an English earl who had fallen on hard times.

Ki, seated next to Jessie, whispered over their dessert of vanilla custard sprinkled with almonds that he guessed the two peacocks they had seen on the lawn outside were worth twenty dollars apiece. At the very least.

Jessie *sshhed* him. And then almost burst into laughter when Willoughby declared expansively, "I have two peacocks I keep on the grounds. Nasty-tempered creatures they are, but I do think they are worth the fifty dollars apiece I was forced to pay for them by the dealer from whom I purchased them. I think they add a certain panache to the place, don't you?"

"Definitely," Ki said solemnly. "When you come right down to it, sir, what is a place like this without peacocks —or panache?"

Willoughby eyed him suspiciously. Then, apparently deciding Ki had been jesting, he let himself indulge in laughter.

Taking a cue from her brother, Matilda simpered softly.

Later, over coffee and brandy served in the sitting room, Willoughby fixed Jessie with a steady stare and proceeded to get down to business.

"I'm sure you know, my dear, there is a great deal of money to be made here in Cripple Creek. But not with our mines shut down."

Jessie sipped her coffee.

"I have spoken to the other mine owners and they are in agreement with me, by and large. I have discussed with them the possibility of ending the strike by whatever means may be necessary or, if that fails, the option of keeping on the Bohunks we've hired in Chicago in their places. I discussed the latter matter with Fred Bolan this morning, as a matter of fact.

"Excuse me, sir," Ki said. "I've heard that term used several times recently by various people. I'm referring to *Bohunks*. What does it mean?"

"It's a term applied to Slavic immigrants in this country. It's rather like our own term for the former slaves we brought to this country. I'm referring, of course, to the term *niggers*."

Ki gritted his teeth.

"Now, then, as I was saying . . ." Willoughby lit a cigar and blew a stream of smoke into the room, which caused Matilda to cough and then to stifle her coughing under the disapproving eye of her brother. "It might be a good thing in the long run to keep the Bohunks in place of the men who have gone on strike."

"Why do you say that?" a curious Jessie inquired.

"Simply because they will work for a low wage and because they are not likely to protest conditions in the mines. They need the work. In this connection, let me say that I have proposed to the Mine Owners' Association members that we reduce the amount of time the workers are allowed to spend in the ice chambers from fifteen minutes per hour to five. In fact, I have eliminated the ice chamber from my own mine.

"Then, too, there are the blowers that are constantly on to circulate the air down below. An enormous expense to operate, as I'm sure you know, Miss Starbuck. They could be run at only certain times. For fifteen minutes each hour, for example."

"I'm not sure such methods would help or be beneficial," Jessie commented. "I've always believed that men work harder and therefore produce more ore if they are treated reasonably and with some consideration."

Willoughby gazed indulgently at Jessie through the cigar smoke that drifted in front of his face. "You have a woman's soft heart."

"You're wrong. I have a *business*woman's keen brain."

"Have it your way." Willoughby drained his brandy glass. "We must, as I'm sure you realize, Miss Starbuck, present a united front in the face of this rebellion that's being led by that rabble-rousing upstart, Dan Calhoun. Anything less will lead to our defeat in this situation facing us."

Jessie understood what Willoughby was saying. It was perfectly clear to her that he expected her to go along with his proposals without objection. "Has the Mine Owners' Association considered compromise as a possible solution to the problem we're all facing?"

"Compromise?" Willoughby spluttered, almost choking on the word. "Did you hear her, Matilda? Miss Starbuck wants to know if we are willing to compromise with the miners."

Matilda stared transfixed at her brother.

"Ridiculous!" he declared.

"Out of the question," Matilda then offered with a sidelong glance at Jessie before dropping her gaze to her custard.

"Talk of compromise is out of the question," Willoughby insisted. "I trust you will come to understand that, Miss Starbuck."

"It's been my experience," Ki said slowly, "that when one gives a little, he often gets a lot in return."

"I agree," Jessie said.

Willoughby stared in disbelief at both of them.

"Of course, I don't intend to be bullied by a man like Dan Calhoun," Jessie stated flatly and firmly.

Willoughby's expression softened. "Good. Very good.

Then you'll stand shoulder to shoulder with the rest of us in our fight with the striking miners?"

"This custard is absolutely delicious, Miss Willoughby," Jessie declared, ignoring the ominous frown her failure to respond to his prodding had brought to Willoughby's suddenly florid face.

★

Chapter 5

Ki stirred in his sleep, but his dreams continued. His dream of Horace Willoughby and Willoughby's sister, Matilda.

In the dream Willoughby was a cat, Matilda a mouse who crept through the elegant house the cat had built with its own paws as if afraid at any moment the dreaded creature would appear and pounce upon her. Silently she moved through the rooms, not daring to squeak or even to touch anything lest the wrath of the cat be brought down upon her.

Ki wanted to speak to her. He wanted to tell her to stand up straight and defy the cat. Make him aware that she was a living being and had her rights. But the words wouldn't come to him. He could only watch helplessly as the cat appeared, opened its jaws, and howled, sending Matilda, the mouse, scurrying into a hole in the sitting room's baseboard from which she peeped out at the now cigar-smoking cat with frightened eyes.

Ki, in his dream, finally found his voice. He let out a roar which caused the cat to vaporize. Then he smiled as

Matilda, no longer a mouse, emerged from the mouse hole and rushed into his arms.

The cat suddenly returned, none the worse for wear. Only now it wasn't the cat. It was Horace Willoughby himself, who began to berate his sister in no uncertain terms for her wanton behavior with what he called "a slant-eyed Jap." There were more wild Willoughby words, all of them ugly, all of them building in intensity until Ki thought he could stand the noise no longer.

He awoke.

The noise continued.

But it was not being made by Horace Willoughby in a dream but by the sound of a very real chorus of men's loud voices drifting through the open window of Ki's room.

He got up, went to the window, and looked out. In the distance—that's where the shouting was coming from. From the vicinity of the Empire Mine. He could not see anymore from where he was; the town's buildings blocked his view. But he could most certainly hear what sounded to him like an incipient riot.

He hurriedly dressed, poured water from a pitcher into a basin on the bureau, and as hurriedly washed. Then he left the room and went to knock on Jessie's door.

She was fully dressed when she opened it. "You heard it, too," she said.

"I heard it. That shouting—there's some kind of trouble brewing at the Empire. I'm going to see what it is."

"Wait. I'll go with you." Jessie disappeared for a moment. When she returned, she was wearing her cartridge belt and Colt.

"I think it would be better if you stayed here," Ki told her.

"Not on your life. I was just coming to get you when you arrived at my door. All that shouting's coming from somewhere near my mine. I have an obligation to go and see what's happening."

79

"You've forgotten what happened to Fred Bolan a while back?"

"No, I haven't forgotten that someone shot him. But the fact that he was shot isn't going to stop me from minding my business, which happens to be the Empire. No, don't argue with me, Ki. I'm going with you or I'm going alone. Which is it to be?"

They went to the mine together.

When they arrived, they found two groups of miners, one consisting of Josip Tito and the men who had come to Cripple Creek with him, the other consisting of Dan Calhoun and the striking miners. The two groups were confronting one another with only a narrow strip of neutral ground separating them. Calhoun's men were lined up in front of the Empire's hoisting works with Calhoun himself standing on top of a loaded ore cart from which he was addressing the men who had taken the strikers' places in the mine.

". . . and they're cheating you men!" he shouted. "They had been paying us three dollars and fifty cents a day. Now they're paying you *two* dollars and fifty cents a day. You're not getting a fair shake from the mine owners!"

"But jobs we have!" Josip shouted back. "Money we make to feed ourselfs and our families. That is not cheating."

"You talk of feeding yourselves and your families," Calhoun responded, changing tactics. "What about us and our families? We have no jobs because of you. Where will the money come from that we can use to feed our families?"

"You go out from mines," Josip countered. "Of your own free will, you go out. We come into mine. Of our own free will. You must not blame us. We did not make you leave the mine."

"But you and all the others like you are killing any chance we might have had to get better pay and better working conditions. You're killing our chances by being willing to work in the mine—and work for a lower wage at that."

One of the men near Josip spoke to him.

"This friend of mine, he is right!" Josip shouted at Calhoun. "Dmitri say we have right to work. He say America, she is free country."

"This country isn't even *yours!*" yelled a man standing beside the ore cart on which Calhoun stood. "Go back where you belong. Go back to your own country!"

Jessie tensed as, for a moment, it seemed that the foreign-born miners were about to surge forward. But she relaxed as Josip managed to hold them in check.

Calhoun pointed at the man who had just spoken, a stocky man with sad eyes below a lined forehead. "You men all know Billy Tippett. You just heard his bitter words. Well, I know and I know that you know that Billy has every right in God's good world to be bitter. He's out here today the same as all you men are to fight for a decent day's pay earned under decent working conditions. Then the mine owners—and I see the owner of the Empire among us this morning—gents, say good day to Miss Starbuck, who's standing back there like she's afraid to show us her face."

"Easy, Jessie," Ki murmured, gripping her arm as she made a move to force herself through the crowd toward Calhoun. "Don't let him bait you."

"As I was just saying," Calhoun continued, his eyes on Jessie, "the mine owners, instead of meeting our demands even halfway, go out and hire themselves a bunch of strike-breakers who don't know us and who don't give a tinker's damn about us."

"You men are fools!" cried Billy Tippett, shaking a fist at Josip and the men with him. "You know some of the owners have closed down their ice chambers so you can't cool off all day long down in the crosscuts. They're talking now, I've heard tell, of shutting down the blowers most of the day on top of everything else. They—"

Calhoun interrupted with, "They don't repair the pumps when they break down so that you're working in hot water up to your hips a whole lot of the time. *Unnecessary!* How much does it cost to repair a pump—or even buy a new one to replace one that's broken down? How much does it cost to keep the blowers on all through a shift?

"A pittance! That's what it costs. But the owners won't spend that pittance. They'd as soon we died like dogs down there in the crosscuts and square sets. They don't give a hoot what happens to us. Not to us"—Calhoun indicated the men on his side— "and not to you boys, either." He pointed to Josip and the men with him. "Dogs come a dime a dozen."

"And there's plenty more to replace the ones what drop dead down in the mines!" Billy Tippett shouted.

"Let us go to work!" Josip demanded. "Get out of our way, you men!"

"You're not going to work today, not a one of you is!" Billy Tippett yelled. "We don't work today; you don't work today, neither."

"I have something to say to all of you!" Jessie called out as she elbowed her way through the crowd until she was standing directly in front of the ore cart, which was Calhoun's platform.

"You heard Mr. Calhoun mention my name a moment ago. I'm Jessica Starbuck, and I own the Empire Mine. Some of you know me. Most of you do not. That is not important. What is important is the way I, through my manager, Fred Bolan, have treated the men who once worked in the Empire and the way we presently treat those of you who work there now.

"Let me ask you this. Is the ice chamber in the Empire closed?"

"No!" chorused several of the Slavs, Josip among them.

"Are the blowers working full-time?"

"Yes!" the same men responded at the tops of their voices.

Jessie gave Calhoun a triumphant over-the-shoulder glance.

"Tell me, Miss Starbuck," he snapped. "How much are you paying those men?" He pointed at the Slavs. "How much per day?"

Jessie hesitated, keenly aware that Calhoun had hit a sore spot in forcing her to admit that she was paying a lower wage to the strikebreakers than she had been paying Calhoun and the other striking miners, a situation which had been bothering her ever since she learned about it from Fred Bolan.

"The lady doesn't answer my question, gents," Calhoun crowed, his arms flung wide. "That's because she's no doubt ashamed of the fact that she's cut the daily wage of her present workers and is paying them a whole lot less than they deserve while they break their backs to make her even richer than she already is."

"You just shut up your mouth, mister!" Josip bellowed as he stepped forward to face Calhoun. "In Chicago, man comes and says to me and my friends I pay you two dollar fifty a day if you come dig in mine for gold. I say thank you very much we will all come quick and we do. So shut you your mouth and let us go to work or we shut your mouth for you. How you like them apples, huh?"

Jessie held up her hands. "Quiet down, please. I have something important to say."

Before she could continue, a surrey driven by Buster drove up. In it sat Horace Willoughby, a dead cigar clamped between his teeth.

"As of today," Jessie continued, "I am reinstating the wage that had been paid to the men who, despite my efforts to be fair to them, went on strike, causing harm to my business interests here. As of today, those of you who are

83

presently employed in the Empire Mine will receive three dollars and fifty cents a day."

A cheer went up from the throats of the Slavs.

When its happy sound had died away, Calhoun said, "This woman—this *mine owner*—wants you to think she had just done you a favor by giving you a rise in wages. She hasn't. Those of us who are on strike are striking in part for a higher wage than the three-fifty per day we were previously paid. We demand a daily wage rate of *four* dollars and fifty cents per day. So you men who are willing to work today and for how many tomorrows, the Lord alone knows, for *three*-fifty per day—"

"Are fools!" Billy Tippett shouted.

"Hold on there!" Willoughby cried as he tossed his cigar away and climbed down from his carriage. With Buster at his side, he forced his way through the crowd to where Jessie was standing. There he halted and, with his hands on his hips, stared up at Calhoun on the ore cart above him.

"What right, sir, have you to prevent these men from doing their day's work?"

"The right of the downtrodden to seek justice," Calhoun answered, the contempt in his voice unmistakably clear.

"You speak of justice, do you? That to me is like the lion speaking of hunger to the antelope it feeds on. You are, I submit, nothing but a fraud. You don't really care what happens to these miners of whom you are the self-appointed leader. You want only the power that comes from convincing other men to do your bidding—in this case, to strike. You want personal glory, Calhoun, not justice. You want to be a hero."

Jessie could see a muscle in Calhoun's jaw jumping and his fists clenching and unclenching. Was he about to leap down from the ore cart and seize Willoughby's thick throat in those strong hands of his?

"It's time you got out of here."

Jessie started at the sound of Ki's voice as he suddenly appeared beside her. "I'm fine," she assured him.

"I came up here to get you and get you away from these hotheads. Something's about to happen. You can feel it in the air. Buster's got a gun strapped around his hips."

"So have I."

"This is not the time nor the place to use it."

"I have no intention of using it."

Ki was about to say something more, but Willoughby's voice stopped him.

"There are ways to put a halt to your troublemaking, Calhoun. If you continue to disrupt the economic life of this community, I shall, let me warn you right here and now, employ any and all means against you and any man who unwisely chooses to stand by your side."

"Don't pay him no mind, Dan," Billy Tippett advised. "He's nothing but a big blowhard is what he is. Not to mention a past master at the slippery art of shady dealing."

"How dare you!" an indignant Willoughby spluttered.

"Oh, it's the truth I'm telling," Tippett insisted. "You and your bully boy Buster there see to it that you buy out any of us should you take to fancying the land on which we've built our homes. To extend your holdings—multiply the land you can legally lay claim to—you buy us out and leave us high and dry."

"I fail to see what is wrong about one man buying land from another man."

"There's not a single thing wrong with one man buying land from another," Tippett said, his head cocked to one side. "But there is a thing or two wrong with *forcing* a man to sell his land to you."

"I do not force anyone to sell land to me," Willoughby protested. "I buy on the open market and pay a fair price."

"You also, some say, sic your dog on those as has land next to what you already own to make them sell out to you.

Take the case of Josh Ransom. You had Buster do for Josh, didn't you? To a faretheewell, you did. When Josh left here for parts unknown after you bought his land from him, he was all but addled from the beating Buster gave him."

"I never did no such thing," Buster stated. "Josh Ransom fell and hurt himself."

"That's what he said after you paid him a *second* visit," Tippett said, wagging a finger at Buster. "What he said to me and others the *first* time around was that you'd beat him so bad he had no choice but to sell out to Willoughby because you told him, Josh did say to me in the hearing of one or two others I could name, that you'd kill him the next time if he didn't."

"This is an outrage!" Willoughby bellowed. "An absolute outrage! Buster would do well to sue you for slander."

"Let him! That'll keep him busy and save me from watching out my windows all the time to see if he is creeping up on me with a gun in his hand like the one he's wearing right now. He'll be too busy with his lawsuit maybe to do that kind of pussyfooting about."

As Buster drew the gun Tippett had just referred to, Ki stepped up to him and deftly wrested the weapon from his hand.

"What the hell—" Buster exclaimed.

"Maybe you'd like to take possession of this gun, Mr. Willoughby," Ki suggested, offering the revolver to the mine owner, who promptly took it from him. "I'm sure you wouldn't want Buster to shoot anyone with it."

"I'm not so sure about that, mister," Tippett interjected. "If you were to ask me, I'd say Buster would as soon shoot a man as beat him senseless like he did to Josh Ransom."

"No more talk!" The words had been yelled by Josip Tito. "We work, not talk." He raised a hand and beckoned to the men with him.

They followed him as he strode toward Calhoun's men,

who were blocking the entrance to the hoisting works.

"Jessie, get out of here!" Ki said. His words were barely spoken when Willoughby tossed the gun in his hand back to Buster, who, gripping the weapon in both hands and crouching, took direct aim at Calhoun.

"Don't!" Jessie cried, going for her own gun.

"You let these men go down into the mine to work," Buster shouted at Calhoun, "or I pull this trigger!"

Jessie's hand halted halfway to her .38. She stood there, her gaze shifting from Buster to Calhoun.

"Mexican standoff," Ki muttered.

Calhoun gazed calmly down at Buster from his position atop the ore cart, seeming not to see the gun in the man's hands.

Buster stared back, not blinking or moving so much as a muscle. "You men want to work, go ahead and work!" he told Josip and the others.

"Go on," Willoughby urged them, gesturing almost frantically. "You heard Buster. You can all go to work now."

Billy Tippett took a step toward Buster, menace alive in his eyes.

"Stand back!" Jessie ordered, her hand dropping to the butt of her gun.

Tippett retreated, glaring at her.

Josip headed for the door of the hoisting works. The other Slavs followed him.

"That's right," an almost jovial Willoughby called out to them. "You're free to go to work. Calhoun's finished. He's smart enough to know when he's licked."

"I'm not licked, Willoughby," Calhoun announced as he jumped down to the ground from the ore cart. "I just don't want any bloodshed."

"You didn't mind shedding Fred Bolan's blood," Willoughby taunted.

"I didn't shoot Bolan."

"I heard otherwise."

"You heard wrong."

"Take your men and get out of here, Calhoun," Buster ordered. "The game's over and you've lost it."

"The game's far from over, Buster," Calhoun countered. "It won't be over till I've played my high card, and I've not seen fit to do that yet."

Jessie watched Calhoun turn his broad back on her and beckon to his men. She continued watching him as he gathered the men together and began to speak earnestly to them in a tone too low for her to hear.

Buster continued to hold his gun on Calhoun—on the man's back.

Willoughby came over to where Jessie was standing and said, "That's the end of the matter."

"Is it?" Jessie wasn't so sure. Calhoun hadn't given up. It seemed to her that he had simply withdrawn his forces for the time being while he planned a new attack—or attacks—on her or another mine owner. She wanted to curse him, but instead found herself admiring him.

"You needn't worry about Calhoun," Willoughby assured her. "Buster effectively called his bluff."

"I don't think he was bluffing."

"I do. You saw what happened when Buster took aim at him. He caved in."

When Jessie said nothing as she continued watching Calhoun, who was still speaking to his men, Willoughby said, "I think you've made a very unwise decision, Miss Starbuck."

"To what do you refer?"

"When I arrived here I heard you tell the Bohunks—"

"Please don't use that degrading word when you speak of my employees, Mr. Willoughby."

"Very well. To get back to what I was about to say to you. You should not, in my opinion, have given in to Calhoun."

"I didn't give in to him."

"Perhaps it doesn't seem that way on the surface and in the short run. But I think that's exactly what you did here this morning, and as I've said, I think it was a mistake. Let me explain."

"Please do."

"You have raised your strikebreakers' daily wage by one dollar. Is that not so?"

"Yes, it is."

"By doing that you have implicitly admitted that the new pay scale I arranged to put in place with the other mine owners and with your manager, Bolan, is inadequate although the strikebreakers were perfectly content with it. It is not a giant step nor a far cry from three-fifty per day to four-fifty per day, which is what Calhoun is demanding we pay him and his strikers. You've taken the first step down that man's rocky road, Miss Starbuck, and I think you will one day deeply regret having done so."

"I think you've misinterpreted my action. If I had really wanted to give in to Mr. Calhoun, I would have fired the miners now working for me and offered to pay him and his men the wage they're demanding—four-fifty per day."

"In any event, Miss Starbuck, you have made a serious error in raising your wage scale beyond that of the rest of us involved in this strike. I believe I mentioned to you at supper last night that it is, in my considered opinion, of the most critical importance that every member of the Mine Owners' Association present a united front in the face of this strike. Having done what you did here today, you have broken that unity which I consider so necessary if we are ultimately to prevail against Calhoun and the other men who have refused to work for us unless and until their absurd demands are met."

"I'm not at all sure that unity should be the primary item on the association's agenda," Jessie declared. "A more important item, it seems to me, is dialogue."

"Dialogue?"

"Between the miners and the mine owners, yes."

"That is an interesting proposition. Yes, most interesting. Are you suggesting, by any chance, that we should negotiate with that rabble?"

"I am. Let us hear what they have to say, and we can tell them our side of the story. That way I think we might well find a way to end this strike. We might be able to come to some sort of mutually satisfactory arrangement."

"Your position, I hasten to tell you, Miss Starbuck, is definitely a minority one. I know of no other mine owner who subscribes to it. The rest of us feel we must do everything in our power to crush this damaging strike and crush it once and for all."

"Mr. Willoughby," Ki said, breaking his long silence, "there is a．saying in the Orient that might be of interest to you."

Willoughby merely stared at Ki.

"The saying goes like this: 'A tree that bends in the wind will not be broken.'"

"You, too, then, I take it, are suggesting the owners should give in to the strikers."

"No, I didn't mean that at all. The saying I quoted merely suggests in a symbolic sort of way that a rigid person is far more likely to suffer insult or injury than is one who knows and practices the delicate art of compromise."

"Oriental nonsense!" Willoughby snarled, turning back to Jessie. "It is not too late to reconsider your position regarding the wages you pay your miners."

"I have reconsidered it, Mr. Willoughby. That is why I increased it. I think at this time and under these difficult circumstances, a median position of paying three-fifty instead of the four-fifty Calhoun wants for his supporters is a suitable compromise as opposed to the two-fifty scale you imposed on the Slavs."

90

"Let me make one thing clear," Willoughby said, his voice low. "I imposed nothing on anyone. I merely made a suggestion to the members of the association. That suggestion was subsequently accepted. *Enthusiastically* accepted."

Without waiting for a response from Jessie, Willoughby turned, beckoned to Buster, and the pair returned to their carriage.

"Lose one, gain another," Ki remarked cryptically.

"What are you talking about?" Jessie asked. Then, as she turned toward him, she knew the answer to her question.

Dan Calhoun, as his men began drifting away in all directions and the last of the Slavs entered the hoisting works, was heading in her direction. Ki had obviously meant that she had lost Willoughby but was about to gain Calhoun. Why did that make her feel pleased? No, more than merely pleased. Happy.

"I thought I should make it my business to thank you for what you did today, Miss Starbuck," Calhoun said as he joined Jessie and Ki.

"I didn't raise my miners' wages as a favor to you, Mr. Calhoun, so there is really no need to thank me."

"Ah, but there is. I saw you go for your gun when that gorilla that tries to walk like a man threw down on me earlier."

Jessie was flustered and not sure what to say. It was true that she had intended to prevent Buster from shooting Calhoun. But she didn't want that act of hers to be misinterpreted.

"I would have done the same thing for anyone," she declared. "I abhor violence, and it seems that Buster was about to initiate it."

"Then you're telling me that we are still enemies, is that it?"

"I'm telling you no such thing. I do not consider you my enemy, Mr. Calhoun. I do consider you impulsive and destructive to your own and others' best interests."

91

"Because I refuse to let myself or the men who think as I do be bullied and coerced by rich mine owners such as yourself?"

"I have never bullied or coerced anyone in my life!" Jessie said sharply, her voice rising.

"Perhaps not directly. But you do belong to the Mine Owners' Association, which I call guilt by association—if you'll forgive the pun.

"And yet you are obviously capable of thinking for yourself. Witness your change of heart about the rate of pay you are willing to offer the strikebreakers you are currently employing. It has occurred to me that perhaps you and I could come to some sort of agreement that would end the strike—at least, insofar as your Empire Mine is concerned."

"When you and your followers are ready and willing to renounce your strongarm tactics, Mr. Calhoun, I shall be ready to talk business with you. In the meantime, I don't think we have anything more to say to each other."

"I'm sorry to see you take that position, Miss Starbuck, I really am. The fact of the matter is, I have a great deal that I would like to say to you. I am not referring only to matters concerning the Empire. Perhaps one day you will have another change of heart, at which time you and I can sit down together, and I will be at liberty at that time to say the things that for now must remain merely on my mind and not spoken aloud. Good day, Miss Starbuck."

Chapter 6

Ki, having risen early the following morning, breakfasted alone in the restaurant across the street from the hotel.

He paid almost as much attention to the buxom woman who served him as he did to the food she placed before him. She was somewhere on the safe side of thirty, he estimated. The cheese that had been grated on top of his scrambled eggs was easily as ripe as she was. The bread he had been served was brown; she was blond and pink-cheeked. His coffee tasted bitter. He suspected the waitress would taste as sweet as the sugar he put in it.

He was almost finished with his meal when she glided across the room and stopped at his table, a coffeepot in her hand. "More coffee, sir?"

"Yes, thank you."

As she refilled his cup, her breasts hovered like two balloons in front of his eyes.

She gave him a smile, and then she and her coffeepot were gone. He drank some of the fresh coffee, wondering if he should—if he dared—give her a kiss as well as a tip when he was ready to leave. He settled for two bits and no kiss.

Outside on the boardwalk, he turned and started down the street. It was too early to wake Jessie. He would take a stroll, he decided. He had gone only two blocks when he saw a vaguely familiar figure up ahead of him. The man was moving slowly away from him. Ahead of the man was a second man. There was no one else in sight. The man who had attracted Ki's attention suddenly began to move faster until he was almost running.

Ki recognized him as he moved into a sunlit patch of the street and something glittered in his hand.

Buster!

"Look out!" Ki yelled to the man he now realized Buster had been stealthily stalking.

The man turned. When he saw Buster almost directly behind him raise his hand, he gave an aborted cry and raised his arms to fend off the blow Buster was about to deliver. He almost succeeded in doing so. Almost but not quite. Buster's right hand descended and glanced off his victim's shoulder, spinning the man around and sending him tottering down the street as if he were drunk.

Ki could now see that Buster did not have something *in* his hand, but *on* it. That something was a silver knuckle-duster. He raced down the street as Buster advanced on his victim.

Just as Buster was about to deliver a roundhouse blow with his metal-knuckled right fist, Ki leaped into the air and landed on Buster's back, knocking him to the ground. Ki was up and ready for him when Buster, swearing lustily, struggled to his feet. Abandoning his original prey, he went for Ki, his right hand ready to strike, sunlight glinting on the thick silver bands that topped the fingers of his right hand.

A wicked weapon, Ki thought. One that could easily break a man's jaw if it landed squarely. Or blind him. Or kill him if it hit his head and caused a concussion.

As Buster, his oaths degenerating into a kind of low growling that rose from the depths of his throat, advanced upon him, Ki began to circle the man, leading him much the way a lion tamer in a circus might lead one of his dangerous beasts.

Buster feinted. Ki withdrew. Buster lunged. Ki's head bent backward, the blow that Buster had aimed at his chin missing him by inches.

Ki stumbled over a large stone lying in the road. As he fought to maintain his balance, Buster took advantage of his momentarily vulnerable position. His metal-enhanced fist struck Ki in the center of his chest. The blow had been aimed at his jaw, but Ki had drawn back in time so that its arc brought it down upon his chest. The wind had been knocked out of him by the strike. He danced backward, his hands raised, seeking an opportunity to repay Buster in kind for what he had just done.

When Buster, momentarily distracted by a spring wagon rumbling past, dropped his guard, Ki made the move he had been waiting to make.

Up went his left leg until it was almost vertical to the ground. He bent backward to help power with his back muscles his hatchet kick that was coming. Then he dropped his foot, heel first, downward and into Buster's face.

Buster screamed in pain. His hands flew up, but he abruptly withdrew them as they touched his face, causing him still more pain.

Ki seized Buster's right arm and held on to it as he ripped the knuckle-duster from Buster's hand and thrust it into his waistband.

Then he let Buster go. Buster stood there, staring at Ki,

blood flowing from his nose. Pain and hate were alight in his narrowed eyes.

Ki, his mind calm, every cell in his body alert, watched Buster carefully.

When the man sprang at him, he stepped nimbly to one side, raised his right leg so that it was parallel to the ground, twisted his body, and slammed his lower leg into the side of Buster's head as he was about to hurtle past, powered as he was by his hate-filled attack that had missed its target.

Ki's blow knocked Buster senseless. He fell to the ground and lay sprawled there as Ki turned to the man Buster had first tried to attack.

"Let's get out of here," he said, taking the wide-eyed man by the arm and shepherding him down the street and around the corner, where he discarded the knuckle-duster he had confiscated from Buster.

"I say, that was a most remarkable performance you put on," the man declared as they turned another corner, leaving no trail for Buster to follow.

"You're all right?" Ki inquired. "He didn't hurt you?"

"No, he didn't, but that's only because you arrived on the scene in the very nick of time, as they say. I don't like to think for a minute of what might have happened had you not come to my aid."

"Why was Buster after you?"

"Is that his name? Buster?"

Ki nodded and repeated his question.

"I don't know really. This all comes as a complete surprise to me. I was just walking down the street minding my own business when there he was, him and those evil silver knuckles of his."

Not satisfied with the man's answer to his question and knowing that Buster must have had some reason for his attack, Ki asked, "What is your business?"

96

"I'm a greengrocer in Denver. Why do you ask?"

"I'm trying to find out why Buster would attack you. What are you doing here in Cripple Creek if your business is in Denver?"

"I came here to look into a matter that has been troubling me for some time."

"What matter?"

"I own stock in the High Stakes Mine here in Cripple Creek."

"I don't follow you."

"I have been receiving repeated requests over a period of time for money from the directors of that mine. They say they need it for such things as new mining equipment or to excavate new shafts or some such thing. I thought it all rather strange, you see, since I have never received any kind of return on my investment in the company, so I decided to come here and try to find out what I could about the mine's operations and to ask why the cash flow went in what I consider to be a highly irregular direction. From the mine's shareholders to the company that owns the mine rather than the other way around, as is customary."

"What you've gotten yourself involved in is what's called an assessment mine."

"Yes, I understand that now, although I did not at the time I bought the shares. Not fully, at any rate. But I've just come from paying a visit to Mr. Willoughby—"

"What's Willoughby got to do with this?"

"Mr. Willoughby is the owner of the High Stakes Mine."

"I see." Ki did indeed see. Or was pretty sure he did. "Go on."

"Well, Mr. Willoughby explained to me that he had the right to assess his shareholder any amount he chose at any time in order to finance the operation of his mine. I was shocked, to say the least. I told him I wanted no part in such a deal. I told him I would not pay another red cent of assessment. He told me that if I chose to take that position, my shares in the High Stakes Mine would automatically become worthless because I had failed to live up to my end of the agreement I signed when I bought the shares which, unhappily, I did not read as carefully as I now know I should have.

"I told him I thought there was something crooked about his whole operation and that I intended to seek legal advice concerning the chances of getting back the money I had already been assessed and had paid. I was on my way to find a lawyer to help me when I was attacked by that man."

"Buster."

"Yes, Buster."

"There's something I think you should know, Mr.—"

"Lendell. Evan Lendell. And your name, sir, is—"

"Ki."

"I'm pleased to meet you, Ki." Lendell offered his hand, and Ki shook it.

"Mr. Lendell, Buster works for Horace Willoughby. My guess is that Willoughby sent him to teach you a lesson. I think he didn't want you going to any lawyer with a complaint about him, so he set out to stop you from doing so. Did Buster threaten you? Tell you to get out of town and forget about a lawyer, for example?"

"No, he didn't. But then he didn't really have much of a chance to, did he? I mean, he had just started to attack me when you came upon the scene."

"Did you go calling on Willoughby at his home?"

"No, he has an office here in town. I went there."

"Where is it?"

Lendell told Ki, and then together they made their way to Willoughby's office, which turned out to be a one-story building on the east side of town. Willoughby's name was lettered in gold on the front window.

As Ki opened the door and ushered Lendell into the office, a bell suspended above the door tinkled.

In response to its summons, a clerk came through a door at the rear of the room. He was wearing a green eyeshade, no coat, and looked to Ki to be nearsighted as he squinted at his visitors.

"Where's Willoughby?" Ki asked without preamble.

"Engaged," was the short answer he received. "I take it you gentlemen have no appointment."

"In there?" Ki pointed at the door through which the clerk had just come.

"I beg your pardon?"

"Is Willoughby in there?"

"Yes, but—"

"Come on, Lendell."

Ki led the way past the protesting clerk and into the office that lay beyond the door.

"What—who—" A startled Willoughby said as he looked up from the papers he had been perusing on his desk. "Oh, it's you. Now don't tell me. I'm good at remembering names. It's Li. No, that's not right. Ki!"

"You also know this fellow right behind me," Ki said, stepping aside so that Willoughby could see Lendell.

"Lendell, I told you to get out of my office and stay out of it," Willoughby snarled. "The door is behind you. Please use it and leave me in peace."

"You'd better send someone to get Buster out of the middle of the street where I left him a little while ago," Ki advised. "Or maybe there's no point to your doing that. Maybe he's been run over by a wagon or two by now."

"What are you talking about?"

"I'm talking about Buster and his knuckle-duster. I'm talking about how I believe you sent him after Mr. Lendell here to keep him from blowing the whistle on you and your High Stakes assessment mine that I'm willing to wager is

99

as worthless as a spider's spit—or the next thing to it, though you've been using it to bilk shareholders like Lendell out of more than just a few dollars."

"You have no right to come barging in here and talking like that to me," Willoughby protested. "I've had nothing but trouble since you and Miss Starbuck came to town. Get out!"

"Not until you buy out Mr. Lendell's position in the High Stakes."

"Buy out—don't be preposterous."

"How much have you been assessed, Lendell?" Ki asked.

"Two thousand dollars."

"Give it back to him, Willoughby."

"I will not."

"If you choose not to, I just might decide to do to you what I did to Buster, who's going to be out of commission for a while, as you'll find out from him sooner or later."

"I owe this man nothing!" Willoughby insisted, trying his best to look brave and succeeding only in looking alarmed.

"You owe Lendell two thousand dollars. Consider yourself fortunate, Willoughby. He's not going to charge you any interest on the money. Nor is he going to sue you for the pain and suffering he experienced at the hands of Buster this morning."

Willoughby gave in. Ki could see the surrender in the man's eyes. He thought it might be followed by tears. It wasn't. Willoughby grudgingly pulled a strongbox out from under his desk. He took a key from his vest pocket and unlocked it. He counted out two thousand dollars and thrust it at a beaming Lendell.

"Now get out of here, both of you!" he said, no longer bellowing, a bull that had been dehorned.

Outside the office, Lendell again shook Ki's hand. "I

am ever so grateful to you, Ki, for all you've done for me."

"Glad I could be of help, Lendell. Now my advice to you is to hop on board the next train that's heading east before Buster has a chance to recuperate and Willoughby decides to put him on your trail again."

"I'll most certainly do that, Ki, I will indeed. But what about you? What if Buster should come after you for having helped me and hurt him, not to mention having forced Willoughby to refund my money?"

"If Buster decides to come after me, he'll find me ready and waiting for him."

Jessie was finishing her breakfast in the restaurant across the street from the hotel when Fred Bolan appeared with another man at his side.

They both made their way over to Jessie's table, where Bolan introduced his companion as Alan Sanders.

"The chemist you suggested we hire," Jessie said to Bolan, recalling the name. "How do you do, Mr. Sanders?"

"Tiptop, Miss Starbuck," the youngish Sanders replied, fairly bubbling over with excitement.

"Sit down, both of you," Jessie said.

"Alan thinks he's on to something," Bolan said when both men were seated at the table. "I could hardly get him to come down to earth long enough to come and talk to you about his findings."

"Have you had success in your search for a process that would allow us to economically extract gold from ore that's mixed with base metals?" Jessie inquired.

"I've made an important breakthrough," Sanders told her as Bolan summoned the waitress and ordered coffee for himself and the chemist. "As you know from Fred's reports," Sanders continued, "I've been working with every raw material except an Irish stew, and sometimes I even contemplated using that to try to get the results we want."

Bolan smiled and said, "Alan's had our millmen filling their amalgamating pans with every witches' brew a man can think of. From mixtures of acids, potash, alum, and what-not to others so arcane I couldn't begin to tell you what all went into them."

"We've even tried using the bark of cedar trees," Sanders said, his coffee ignored. "It didn't do the job any more than anything else we tried did. We just could not find the proper agent that would allow the extraction of every last ounce of gold from other than pure ore."

"I suggested he try sagebrush," Bolan said, only half-joking.

"I confess I was about ready to throw in the towel," Sanders admitted, fidgeting in his seat across from Jessie. "I was even ready to risk Starbuck Enterprises' money on one or more of the process-peddlers that have been haunting the Empire office as well as every other mine office in the area. I thought maybe they really did know a successful process, as all of them unfailingly claim to. I was that desperate, Miss Starbuck."

"I've heard that some success has been achieved in extracting nearly all the gold from ore in the Comstock Lode mines," Jessie remarked. "After crushing, stamping, and agitating the ore in a mixture of water, mercury, salt, and bluestone copper sulphate, they had quite good results as far as their yields went."

"I know that," Sanders said. "We tried the same process here initially, but the Western ores are far too adulterated in most cases with sulphur, copper, zinc, and lead so that the process just won't work as effectively on them."

"They are," Bolan interjected, "'rebellious,' to use the millman's word for such impure ores."

"What about steeping the ore in tanks of chlorine gas?"

102

Jessie inquired. "Hasn't there been some success with that process?"

"True, there has been," Sanders admitted. "But it's not anywhere near one hundred percent effective nor is it a cost-effective process, by and large. What we needed, Miss Starbuck—what we wanted—was a process which would allow us to get every last bit of gold out of mine tailings which are now worthless, although they do contain some residual gold which we cannot now extract from them using our present processes."

"Alan thinks he may finally have found a way to do just that," Bolan said.

"Stumbled upon it, would probably be a better way to put it," Sanders said modestly.

"Tell me what you've discovered," Jessie said, beginning to share the chemist's enthusiasm, which she was finding contagious.

"As I've said, I've been experimenting with all kinds and manner of processes. None of them worked. Until now. Just yesterday I hit on the idea of dissolving gold in a weak solution of sodium cyanide and then running the solution through beds of fine zinc shavings."

"Hold on a moment, Mr. Sanders," Jessie said. "I'm no chemist nor am I a metallurgist. So perhaps you'll explain to me how what you've just described will benefit us."

"It's actually quite simple," Sanders said, his eyes alight. "What happened was this. During the process I just described, the gold adhered to the zinc shavings. What I did then was to heat the two metals. When I did that, they separated. What all that means, Miss Starbuck, is that the process I've developed, when put into practice on a much larger scale than my small experimental one, may, if it works on that larger scale, allow us to retrieve virtually one hundred percent of the gold the Empire Mine's now worthless tailings contain."

"That sounds marvelous," Jessie declared. "Truly marvelous. Almost magical, in fact. You're to be congratulated, Mr. Sanders."

"Don't congratulate me yet," Sanders said. "What I've done—it may turn out to be merely some kind of fluke. When we try it on a larger scale under carefully controlled conditions—well, quite frankly, there's no real guarantee that it will work."

"But you do plan to try it on a larger scale, don't you?" Jessie asked.

Sanders glanced at Bolan, who said, "That's where we may find a fly in the ointment. To set things up so that Alan's cyanidation process, as he calls it, can be properly tested, we will have to incur considerable expense."

"What expenses are involved?" Jessie asked.

"Well, to start with, we will have to construct one or more cyanide vats on a large enough scale to process the sands from our piles of tailings. We will have to import cyanide in fairly large quantities from a firm in Germany called I.G. Farbenindustrie, A. G. We—"

Jessie held up a hand. "Have you put down any figures? Made any profit projections, however theoretical they may be at this point?"

"I have." Bolan reached into the inner pocket of his jacket, pulled out a paper, and handed it to Jessie.

He and Sanders remained silent then as Jessie carefully studied the profit-and-loss statement Bolan had prepared for Sanders's cyanidation process. She spent a good ten minutes going over the figures, checking the mathematics, raising questions which one or the other of the two men answered and voicing an occasional objection which they resolved to her complete satisfaction.

"Go to it, gentlemen," she said finally, handing the paper back to Bolan.

Sanders let out a cry of unrestrained delight, which

caused other diners in the restaurant to start and stare nervously at him.

Jessie said, "If your calculations are correct, Fred, and if, more important, Mr. Sanders's cyanidation process proves to be not just a fluke but a truly viable method of extracting nearly every bit of gold from previously discarded ore, then I think we should double our initial retrieval operation as soon as possible."

"Let's fervently hope it works," Sanders said in an uncharacteristically somber tone of voice.

"We'll keep our fingers crossed," Jessie said.

After bidding good-bye to Bolan and Sanders outside the restaurant, Jessie crossed the street on her way back to the hotel lobby. She had just reached the door that led to the lobby when it swung open and she almost collided with Dan Calhoun, who was coming through it.

As she stepped back, Calhoun said with a grin, "I'm glad I ran into you, Miss Starbuck. I was just inside asking the desk clerk did he know your whereabouts since there was no answer when I knocked on your door. He told me you had gone out, but where to he claimed not to know."

"What is it you want with me, Mr. Calhoun?"

"I thought since you and I don't seem to be able to get along all that well together, I'd introduce you to someone who could perhaps help you understand the plight of the miners who are on strike better than I can. I'm talking about one of your own employees—one of your *former* employees."

"I hope you are not blaming me for the fact that this man you speak of—"

"His name's Billy Tippett."

"—is a former employee. *I* didn't order him to leave his job and go on strike, nor did anyone else in my employ."

"Ah, here we go again," Calhoun said with a melodramatic roll of his amber eyes. "Peace, please, Miss Star-buck. Or, if not peace, at least a truce for the time being. What do you say?"

"I say you are a most persistent man, Mr. Calhoun."

"That I am, that I most definitely am. It's the only way to get what one wants out of the world." Calhoun met Jessie's gaze with a stare of such sensual intensity, she was forced to look away from him for a moment. "Now," he continued, "if you'll just walk along with me, Miss Star-buck, we'll go and pay a call on Billy and his wife, who is awaiting the arrival of their first child, by the way. It's not far. A few blocks. They live on the edge of Paupers' Patch."

"Paupers' Patch? A rather colorful name for a neighbor-hood, isn't it?"

"Paupers' Patch is more of a slum than it is what you could call a neighborhood. Shall we go?"

Calhoun offered Jessie his arm but she didn't take it.

They arrived at the Tippett home less than ten minutes later. It was more a hovel than a home, set among a cluster of similar dwellings, none of them looking too sturdy, all of them looking rather worn and weary. No curtains hung in the windows of any of the houses except Tippett's, where a frilly flowered piece of muslin covered the spar-kling panes. In the tiny yard of the house a few geraniums grew, jauntily red against the few scraps of green grass that were visible.

Calhoun knocked on the door, which was opened by a plain and very obviously pregnant woman wearing a faded apron. Her auburn hair was bound up on top of her head. It matched the color of her eyes. She smiled when she saw Calhoun. She frowned when she saw Jessie.

"This is Miss Starbuck, May," Calhoun told her. "Is Billy to home?"

"Where else would Billy be, Dan? What does a man do

when he has no work? He sits to home and sulks, that's what he does."

"May, darlin', be happy that Billy isn't downtown in a tavern lifting too many pints."

"Go on with you, Dan Calhoun," May said sternly, but she couldn't help smiling. "You know my Billy's as sober as Sunday."

"Men change, May. Best you keep a close eye on that husband of yours. May we come in?"

"The house is a fright. I'm in the midst of cleaning it."

"I really want Miss Starbuck to meet and talk to Billy, May," Calhoun pleaded.

"Very well, then. Come in."

Calhoun waited until Jessie had crossed the threshold and then followed her into the dim interior of the house. They found Billy Tippett dozing in front of the stone hearth with his feet up on a stool. He started at the sound of their entrance, blinked, and then got quickly to his feet.

"My word," he declared, "what's *she* doing here?"

"I'm not sure myself, Mr. Tippett," Jessie said. "I was asked to come by Mr. Calhoun. If I'm not welcome—"

"I'll make a pot of tea," May volunteered to soothe troubled waters.

"Sit down," Tippett said, drawing up a wooden chair for Jessie.

When she was seated, he returned to his chair.

Calhoun seated himself on the stool Tippett had been using as a footrest and said, "I asked Miss Starbuck to come here today, Billy, so you could tell her about Willoughby's offer to buy your land."

Tippett's brow wrinkled. "Ah, that. Well, there's not a whole lot to tell when you come right down to it, is there, Dan?"

"I recall mention being made at the confrontation at the

Empire," Jessie said, "about Willoughby wanting to purchase your land, Mr. Tippett."

"He wants to buy it, he does."

"Tell him, Billy," Calhoun prodded.

"You see, miss, Willoughby owns most of the land in Paupers' Patch as it is. He wants to own more. My little bit very much included. There's rich ore underneath where we're sitting right this minute, miss. Willoughby means to mine it all before he's through."

"Did he make you a good offer?"

Tippett exchanged glances with Calhoun and then answered, "He did not. He offered May and me seventy-five dollars."

"Seventy-five dollars for the whole kit and caboodle," May said, returning with a teapot and a tray of cups. "That money was supposed to pay us for the land and the house that sits on it as well." She placed the cups on a table and then went and got a pitcher of milk. "Now, I'll grant you that this house isn't much. But it is a roof over our heads and it is worth something to Billy and me."

As May proceeded to pour the tea, her husband said, "There's no place in the West or even the world, for that matter, that a man can get to buy land and build himself a house—"

"A home," May said.

"—for seventy-five dollars. None at all."

Jessie took the cup of tea May handed her.

"It's highway robbery, his offer is," Tippett said.

"But Willoughby knows he's got Billy and May over a barrel," Calhoun said, accepting a cup of tea from May. "Willoughby has ways of getting what he wants."

"Not nice ways they are, neither," Tippett muttered.

"Will you take milk, Miss Starbuck?" May asked. "I'm afraid we've no sugar. Sugar costs twenty cents the pound, and that's a bit dear for us at this hard time in our lives."

"I like it black, Mrs. Tippett, thank you."

"We're ever so afraid of what Mr. Willoughby might do to us if we don't sell out to him," May lamented as she sat down and wrapped her hands, as if to warm them, around her cup of steaming tea. "Mr. Willoughby's willful and he means to have what he wants. He'll not let anyone stand in his way of getting it, he won't. But my man here, he's a stubborn one, he is. He won't sell."

"Stubborn it is, am I?" Tippett said to his wife. "Would you have me be spineless, May? Would it make you happy to see me down on my knees licking Willoughby's boots to thank him for his generous offer of seventy-five dollars for our hearth and home?"

"Billy, don't be upset," May said softly. "No, I wouldn't want you giving in to the man. But it's fearful I am of what he might do if you don't sell. It's awful fearful I am, and that's the plain truth of the matter."

"I vow by all the saints in heaven," Tippett declared fervently, "I'll not let happen to me what happened to Josh Ransom."

Jessie said, "I've heard that name before." Then, remembering, she said, "It was mentioned at the mine the day of the confrontation."

"Josh Ransom was a miner in Willoughby's Bluebell Mine," Calhoun reminded Jessie. "He lived right here in Paupers' Patch. He claimed Buster beat him within an inch of his life after he refused to sell out to Willoughby."

"That beating changed Josh's mind in a hurry," Tippett said bitterly. "He sold out fast enough after that. Then he left town with his wits scrambled, he did. No one's seen hide nor hair of him or his family since."

"It's not just myself I'm afraid for," May said plaintively. "It's for the babe on the way that I'm fretting mostly." Her hands left her teacup and came to rest on her bulging belly.

"Miss Starbuck," Calhoun said, rising and beginning to pace back and forth in the small room, "you're probably wondering why I wanted you to hear all this from Billy and May."

"No, Mr. Calhoun, I'm not wondering why. I know why. It's perfectly clear to me that you think I should not be taking the same position as that of Mr. Willoughby because you don't think he is a reputable man."

Calhoun, taken aback by Jessie's response, could only stare at her.

"My position on the strike you men are waging," she continued, "should not in any way be construed as an endorsement of any of Mr. Willoughby's policies or tactics."

"Then you agree with me that Willoughby's wrong in what he's been doing—in effect stealing property from families like the Tippetts," Calhoun said, a note of hope in his voice.

"I most certainly disapprove of any such tactics, no matter who practices them."

Calhoun looked relieved. "Do you also disapprove of the other things he has done in his mine of late? Things like turning off the blowers for most of the workday so that his strikebreakers can barely breathe down in his mine? Or his elimination of the ice chamber that all mine owners—until now—have maintained for the well-being and comfort of their workers? Or his refusal to repair or replace broken pumps so that his workers must sometimes work in hip-deep water? Do those things strike you as right and proper?"

"They do not. But let me remind you, Mr. Calhoun, that no such conditions exist in my mine. In addition, let me remind you that I have just increased the daily wage my workers earn."

110

"You're missing the point, Miss Starbuck," Calhoun said.

Jessie bristled but she said nothing.

Calhoun continued, "By aligning yourself with Willoughby, who, as we all know, is the dictatorial power behind the Mine Owners' Association, you are strengthening his hand and implicitly endorsing the actions he has taken —and persuaded others to take—to reduce his expenses and increase his profits."

"What Dan is saying is the truth, miss," Tippett said. "Now, you're a smart lady. I'll wager you can see that if Willoughby wins—if we give in and go back to work— then we'll be going back to work in the mines the way they are now, which will kill many of us before we're forty. Him and the other owners will maintain conditions and wages just the awful way they are right now."

Jessie thought of the contemptuous way in which Willoughby had spoken of the "Bohunks" he was employing. She thought of his apparent disregard for their welfare, which had bothered her during the supper at the Willoughby home. She knew Tippett and Calhoun were right.

"If you broke with Willoughby," Calhoun was saying, "it would help us win our battle for a decent wage and decent working conditions. You'd have cracked his prized united front against us."

"Would you consider doing that for us?" Tippett asked hopefully.

"You wouldn't be doing it just for Billy and the other men who are on strike," May said somewhat timidly. "You'd be doing it for the benefit of the wives and children of those men as well."

Jessie said, "I have to repeat that I've already taken steps away from the position held by Willoughby and others. The working conditions in the Empire are far better

111

than they are elsewhere at present and the wages are higher."

May said, "The men working in your mine and their families as well will bless you for what you've done, Miss Starbuck. They'll remember you in their prayers."

"I hope you all can understand that I'm also concerned about the men who are now working in my mine," Jessie said. "My manager hired a number of them, as you know. I don't want to discharge them at this point if I can avoid doing so. They came here all the way from Chicago, and they need their jobs."

"We're not asking you to fire those men at this point," Calhoun said. "We're asking only that you let it be known that you are willing to negotiate with us to settle the strike."

"I thought you were asking me to hire back the men who worked in the Empire before they went on strike."

Calhoun shook his head. "We all go back to work at the same time in all the mines in Cripple Creek or none of us goes back."

"I see. I'll talk to some of the other owners and let them know I'm considering negotiating an end to the strike. I'll try to persuade as many of them as I can to do the same."

"At this point, there's something we ought to say to the lady, Dan," Tippett said in a voice almost too low for Jessie to hear.

The two men stared at each other for a long moment before Calhoun turned to Jessie and said, "What Billy is getting at is the fact that if you do go up against Willoughby by being willing to negotiate with us, you might be putting yourself at risk."

"I'm not sure I follow you."

"We told you about what happened to Josh Ransom," Tippett reminded Jessie.

"You don't really believe that Willoughby would attempt to do me harm if I take a stand opposed to his own, do you?"

Neither Calhoun nor Tippett answered her question. Which was, she realized, an ominous answer in and of itself.

Chapter 7

"I want to thank you for coming with me today," Calhoun told Jessie as they stood outside Tippett's house. "I also want to thank you for seeing things the miners' way."

"Not so fast, Mr. Calhoun. I never said I saw things the miners' way—not everything, certainly. I agreed to negotiate with the men through you. I don't believe, for example, that four-fifty per day is a reasonable rate of pay."

"Well, I'll let that go for now," Calhoun remarked amiably. "I certainly don't want to make a wrong move at this juncture that might make you turn on me and once again begin to think of me as—what did you call me the other day? I've forgotten."

"I haven't. I called you a common hoodlum, Mr. Calhoun, and you were."

"But now?"

"Now I'm prepared to say only that you may possess one or two redeeming qualities."

"Such as?"

"I'm quite convinced that you have the interests of the miners at heart. I think, too, that you are genuinely concerned about bettering their lot."

"I really am, you know. It's unfortunate that sometimes a man must behave like a common hoodlum in order to accomplish his goals in the face of bull-headed opposition—" Calhoun stopped in midsentence. "Uh-oh," he said with a sheepish grin. "I almost put my foot in my mouth again, didn't I?"

"Both feet. Good day, Mr. Calhoun."

As Jessie set out on her way back to the hotel, she resisted the urge to glance over her shoulder to see if Calhoun was still where she had left him. Was he watching her? What difference did it make? She wished she could feel neutral toward the man, but she seemed unable to do so. He either angered or attracted her. There was a magnetism about him that drew her to him, albeit resisting all the way. Nevertheless, there it was and here she was walking away from him when what she really wanted was to stay with him, to hear him ask her to—

She deliberately derailed her train of thought and concentrated instead on her next move. She wouldn't go directly back to the hotel, she decided. She would first of all pay a call on Cornelius Vandam, president of Vandam Mining Company, whose office, she recalled, was only two blocks from where she was right now.

She turned right at the next corner, walked down a block, made a left turn, and soon came to the office of Vandam Mining Company.

Once inside its spacious reception room, she asked the young woman seated at one of the new typewriting machines if Mr. Vandam was in his office.

"Yes, ma'am, he is. Who shall I say wishes to see him?"

"Jessica Starbuck."

The receptionist rose and disappeared. When she returned a few minutes later, she announced that Mr. Vandam would be most pleased to see Miss Starbuck. "If you'll come this way."

Jessie followed the secretary to Vandam's office, where Vandam was awaiting her.

"What a surprise—what a very pleasant surprise, Jessie!" he exclaimed, rising from behind his desk to shake hands with her. "To what do I owe this wholly unexpected visit?"

"It's good to see you again, Cornelius. It's been a long time."

"Sit down, Jessie, do. Yes, it has been a long time. It was a year ago, wasn't it, that we last met?"

"That's right."

"I do wish you'd grace this town and us with your presence more often. We mine men grow old and grizzled in the absence of lovely and charming women such as yourself."

"I'm not sure you'll be glad to see me when I tell you why I've come, Cornelius."

Vandam seated himself behind his desk and folded his hands across his ample girth. "Why did you come, Jessie? I know it's not just to brighten an old man's day."

"Cornelius, I think you and I and the other mine owners ought to sit down with the strikers and do some serious bargaining to try to settle the strike."

Vandam's eyes widened and his eyebrows rose. "You always were one for getting right to the point and not mincing words, my dear. But what you are proposing—I'm not at all sure such a plan is feasible. It is far more likely to be, it does seem to me, little more than a pleasant fancy."

"Why do you say that, Cornelius?"

"Because of Horace Willoughby, that's why. He's adamant about holding out against the strikers until, as he put it to me recently, 'hell freezes over and we can all skate on the ice.' You see, he insists that the strikers are only out to bleed us all dry. He won't be happy to hear what you're proposing."

"Are you in accord with Willoughby's position?"

"There's no doubt that cutting the miners' pay will show up on the plus side of our ledgers."

"What about Willoughby's idea of reducing the time the blowers are kept on in the crosscuts and shafts and his having removed the ice chamber from his mine?"

"That doesn't please me very much nor do I intend to do as he has done in those respects. What would it save? Pennies a day?"

"I agree with you. What we would risk losing by such actions would be the morale of our work force. The men wouldn't work any harder than they absolutely had to under such stressful conditions of the kind Willoughby is imposing upon them in his operation. I for one think it's a shortsighted plan, to put it kindly. Actually, I think it's an absurd plan. A plan which will, in the long run, do us far more harm than good."

"Well, Jessie, you know Willoughby. He's a man who probably still has the first dollar he earned. He's a man who, I swear to you, could squeeze blood from a stone."

"What do the other owners think of his plans?"

"Well, Otis Delaney is going along with Horace. So is Barry Barnett."

"What about Virgil Compton?"

"I haven't heard him raise any serious objections. But then, I wouldn't expect Virge to."

"What do you mean by that? Is Virge of a similar mind as Willoughby?"

"No, as a matter of fact, he isn't. Virge is a man with a heart as big as a barn. But he's also a man who has had some business problems of late. You probably heard about them."

"I heard that he had a cave-in in his mine, yes."

"That and some other setbacks around the same time left him strapped for cash. Mel Baker at the bank wouldn't lend him another red cent. He was at that same time already into the bank for close to fifty thousand. So what did Virge do? He did the only thing he could do. He went to Willoughby, who's got more money than he knows what to do with, and Willoughby came up with the money he needed. At fourteen percent interest, incidentally. Now, given all that, do you think Virge is going to go head to head with his benefactor over this strike business?"

"I see what you mean."

"Willoughby, as you no doubt know, is a shrewd man. He's bought up more than fifty percent of the outstanding shares in Otis Delaney's mine—on the sly—so Otis tends to dance to whatever tune Willoughby decides to play. As for Barry Barnett, well, I don't mean to be uncharitable, but Barry's a fellow who likes life nice and easy. He doesn't like trouble. So he went along with Willoughby sooner than buck the tide. I don't think Barry cares that much what happens just so long as he can keep on making money one way or the other."

"What about you, Cornelius?"

Vandam sighed. "I'm probably in the best position of all of us—present company excepted—where Willoughby's carrot-and-stick game's concerned. I've steered clear of him over the years, by and large. But like Virge, I borrowed money from him some time back, but that note's just about paid off as of now, so I can go up against him without the risk of losing my shirt to him."

"*Will* you go up against him? With me?"

"No, Jessie, I won't. I'll tell you why. I have to live in this town. Unlike you, I have to get along with the people

118

on a daily basis, Willoughby very much included. But I will do this. I'll have a talk with Virge and Delaney and Barnett and one or two others to see if they might consider sitting down and talking with the strikers."

"Thank you, Cornelius. Thank you very much."

"Mind you now, I may not get anywhere. But it does seem to me that if I can get even one of them to help us try to settle this strike, Willoughby might have to throw in the towel rather than make trouble for us. I know for a fact that early on, Delaney was ready to offer the miners four dollars a day, but when Willoughby got wind of that, he put the kibosh on it and Delany backed off."

"Maybe between the two of us we can return things to normal here in Cripple Creek. I for one certainly do hope so. I don't like the mood of the strikers. I think we're facing trouble ahead, serious trouble maybe."

"I agree."

"You'll let me know what the other owners have to say, won't you, Cornelius? I'm staying at the Nugget Hotel."

"I'll let you know as soon as I can, Jessie."

When Jessie returned to the hotel, she found Ki waiting for her in the lobby.

"Have you had breakfast?" she asked him.

"I have. I was up early. Where've you been?"

"Dan Calhoun took me to visit Billy Tippett and his wife."

"The name's familiar—Tippett's, I mean."

"He was the man who accused Willoughby of trying to force him off his land during the confrontation at the Empire."

"I remember now. Why did Calhoun take you there?"

"He wanted me to hear Tippett's opinions of Willoughby—and his fears concerning Willoughby's tactics."

"I find that interesting since I got involved today with

something Willoughby's man, Buster, was up to."

"Oh?"

"I ran into Buster as he was in the process of trouncing a fellow with the help of a silver knuckle-duster."

"So you, of course, sided with the underdog."

"You didn't for a minute think I'd sided with Buster, did you?" Ki grinned. "It was a short fight. Buster lost it."

"Willoughby put Buster up to the attack?"

"Apparently so, although he later denied doing so. It seems that Willoughby's been running a deal whereby he sells shares in a mine he owns named the High Stakes, and then he makes periodic demands on his shareholders for money that he claims is needed to keep the mine operating or to make improvements or some such thing."

"An assessment mine."

"Exactly."

"There's nothing necessarily wrong with such an operation. In the early days of the Empire, when the mine was not yet profitable, we assessed stockholders semi-annual fees to capitalize the operation."

"But according to the man I met, Willoughby has never paid a dividend. He just milks shareholders. They pay but he's the only one it would seem who profits from the High Stakes."

"He may well have had no intention of ever giving his stockholders any return on their investments. It's happened before. Someone buys a played-out mine, sells shares to unwary people, and then makes as much money out of them as he can by means of assessments before flying the coop and leaving the shareholders holding stock in a worthless piece of real estate."

"The man I met, I learned, was about to make trouble for Willoughby. I took him to Willoughby's office, where, as I said, he claimed he didn't send Buster to strongarm the fellow. To make a long story short, I got him to give back the money he had bilked from the man.

"Now tell me about your visit to Tippett's."

Jessie did so, and when she finished, Ki said, "Maybe Tippett ought to sell out to Willoughby just to be on the safe side if he's so worried about the well-being of his wife and himself."

"He won't do that, I gather. He's a stubborn man. A proud man, too. He won't give in to Willoughby's thinly disguised threats, and I can't say I blame him. I'd probably do the same thing in his place."

"And probably buy yourself a bushelful of trouble in the process."

"Perhaps." Jessie was silent for a moment and then said, "I promised Dan Calhoun that I would sit down and negotiate with the miners. I also promised him I'd talk to some of the other owners and see if they would agree to do the same thing in an effort to put an end to the strike."

"I would have thought you would have been more likely to try to kill Calhoun than to agree to cooperate with him."

"He's just doing what he thinks is right. I can't entirely disagree with the position he's taken, although I think his wage demand is outrageous. But the basic point here is the parties involved have got to find a way to settle their differences without any more violence.

"To that end, I paid a call on Cornelius Vandam, who owns a large mine in Cripple Creek." Jessie proceeded to give Ki an account of what she and Vandam had discussed.

"Well, it sounds to me like you're making progress in attempting to end the strike. But aren't you going about it in a rather indirect way?"

"What do you mean?"

"I mean that, based on what Vandam told you and what we already know, Willoughby's apparently the prime mover in this shindig. It seems to me that he's the one you ought to try to win over to your way of thinking. Maybe you ought to think about trying to beard the lion in his den, so to speak."

"It's odd that you should say that, Ki. On my way back here just now, I'd considered the possibility of having a talk with Willoughby in the hope of being able to get him to reconsider his stand. But I decided I would probably be wasting my time."

"Well, you won't know that for sure until and unless you give it a try, will you?"

Jessie, after a moment's thought, said, "I'll have a talk with him."

"Be careful when you do. Willoughby and his assessment mine, his bringing in the strikebreakers, his use of Buster to help him get what he wants—that man's got more crooked cards up his sleeve than any Mississippi riverboat gambler."

Jessie drove to Willoughby's office but was told by his clerk that Willoughby had not come in that day.

"Is he at home?"

"I really couldn't say."

Jessie decided to drive to Willoughby's home in the hope that she would find him there. What had Ki said? Something about bearding the lion in his den.

Later, as she knocked on Willoughby's door, she heard loud voices coming from inside the house. A man's and a woman's.

She was hearing Matilda's voice, she realized, and then, after another moment, she recognized Josip Tito's voice. Now, what was he doing here of all places, and what was it that had led to the shouting match that was taking place inside?

The sound of the shouting increased as a maid opened the door in response to Jessie's knock.

"I'd like to see Mr. Willoughby, please."

"The master is not at home."

"Then I'll talk with Miss Willoughby, if I may."

"One moment, please." The maid closed the door. When she reopened it a little later, the shouting had stopped. "Miss Willoughby will see you."

Jessie followed the maid into the sitting room, where she found Matilda Willoughby and a florid-faced Josip Tito.

"What do *you* want?" Matilda snapped.

Taken aback but trying not to show it, Jessie answered, "I wanted a word with your brother, but since he is not available, I thought I would ask you where he is so that I might go there and speak to him."

"I have no idea where my brother is."

"*I* have no idea where is my friend, Stanislaus," Josip said. "Or my friend, Vladimir. Or my other friends who go to work in Bluebell Mine and do not come out again."

"I have told you over and over again," Matilda said with little patience, "that I know nothing about your friends or where in the world they might be!"

"Miss, maybe you know something, yes?" Josip asked Jessie.

"What is it that's troubling you, Mr. Tito?"

"My friends, they go yesterday morning like always to work in Bluebell Mine. They not come home last night. The wife of Stanislaus, she come to me to say her husband has disappeared. So it is with other men in Bluebell Mine. They go down. They not come up."

"Have you made inquiries about them?"

Josip frowned. "What is this 'inquiries'?"

Jessie explained.

"Yes, I go to mine. Speak to foreman. He say he have no thing to say to me. He tell me go away before I shoot you. Yes, he have gun. Is fine thing, yes? What for does

123

foreman need gun? I ask you, miss. Pick and shovel, they good to have in mine. But gun?"

"What, if anything, do you know about this, Miss Willoughby?" Jessie asked.

"Nothing. I know nothing about it. I told that to this man when he came here asking about his friends. I wish you would both go away and leave me in peace. If you have anything to say to Brother, come back when he is here."

"When will that be?" Jessie asked.

"I don't know," Matilda wailed, ready to burst into tears.

"Is he at the mine?"

"I told you I don't know where he is or when he'll let those men out—" Matilda's hands flew up to cover her mouth.

"What were you about to say, Miss Willoughby?" Jessie pressed. "What men were you talking about? Is your brother holding Mr. Tito's friends prisoner in his mine?"

"I don't know and I am not qualified to discuss Brother's business dealings with anyone. I do not have the head for it."

Jessie, listening to Matilda, thought she had suddenly begun to sound like a little girl.

"Brother always said I had no flair for figures. He was right. I know nothing of bonds or debentures or esoteric things such as that. Brother tends to such things."

"Miss Willoughby, stick to the point," Jessie said a trifle sharply. "You said something to the effect that you don't know when your brother will let the men out when I asked you if he was at his mine. What did you mean by that?"

"Nothing. I meant nothing."

Josip seized Matilda by the shoulders and began to shake her. "You know more than nothing I think. Tell it!"

Jessie quickly stepped forward and removed Josip's hands from Matilda's shoulders.

"I mind my own business," Matilda said in a voice that had suddenly turned harsh. No longer speaking in the voice of a child, she added, "Brother minds his own business and I mind mine. We find that a perfectly satisfactory arrangement. Now I have things to tend to. The maid will show you both out."

Matilda went to a bell rope and pulled it.

The maid materialized and, in obedience to a peremptory gesture of Matilda's, showed Jessie and Josip out of the house.

"That woman, she know something about Vladimir and Stanislaus and my other friends who work for Willoughby," Josip insisted darkly once the door had closed behind him and Jessie.

"I'm inclined to agree with you, Mr. Tito. The question is, what exactly does she know?"

Josip shook his head. "I do not know."

"I have an idea. I might be wrong, but I think I know where your friends are. Do you have a carriage here?"

"I walk here. No money for carriage."

"Would you like to ride into town with me while I look into this matter of your missing friends?"

"I would, yes. Where do we go to find them?"

Once in town, Jessie drove to the Cripple Creek Mining Exchange and led Josip into the building. She asked the shirtsleeved man behind a tall desk if he could tell her where she could find out which stocks had been most actively traded on the exchange during the past week. He directed her to an office on the building's second floor. There, she was given a handwritten list of four stocks which, the man who had prepared the list for her stated, "were hot numbers all week long."

Willoughby's Bluebell Mine headed the list as the stock most heavily traded during the past week.

"Can you tell me who did most of the recent buying of Bluebell shares?" Jessie asked the harried man, giving him a winning smile which effectively silenced the objection he had been about to make to her request.

He consulted a file and then said, "Horace Willoughby."

"Thank you. You've been most kind. It's always a pleasure to do business with such a capable and obliging gentleman as yourself."

Outside on the street again, Josip gripped Jessie's arm. "Miss, you tell me now what is all this. I do not understand."

Jessie told him, concluding with "I can't prove anything but that's what I believe has been and is still going on. Now, the next step obviously is to find Horace Willoughby and tell him what we suspect. I suggest we try the Bluebell Mine."

"Let us go there quick."

They did, and when they reached the mine, Jessie braked and got out of the carriage. She and Josip were crossing a dusty expanse of ground between two rows of wooden buildings when Josip muttered, "There is Willoughby."

"Come on," Jessie said, and Josip followed her as she hurried toward the mine owner in the distance.

But before she reached him, he entered a smaller building on one side of the hoisting works which bore a small sign which read: OFFICE.

Less than a minute later, as Jessie was about to open the door of the office, the sound of Willoughby's voice coming through an open window stopped her. She stood there, listening.

". . . don't care how long they have to be kept down there," Willoughby was saying. "We send them food, don't

126

we? We see to it that they have water. We've promised to pay them an extra fifty cents per day, haven't we? What the hell more do they want?"

"Sir," someone said, "they say they do not get sufficient food and only a little water. They say now that they don't care about the additional money you've agreed to pay them. They just want to be able to leave the mine."

"Well, you tell them for me that they aren't leaving the mine until I give them permission to do so. Now, I don't want to hear any more complaints. As my mine manager, Frazier, it's your job to handle them. Don't bother me anymore with the whining of that sorry lot of Bohunks."

Jessie opened the door and stepped into the office with Josip right behind her.

Willoughby, who had his back to the door, spun around. Seeing Jessie, he frowned. "What do you want?"

"I see we have dispensed with the social niceties," Jessie commented. "Well, so be it. What I want, Mr. Willoughby, is for you to make known the fact that you have recently discovered an additional source of gold in your mine."

Willoughby's jaw dropped. He tried to speak. Couldn't. He stared at Jessie, obviously dumbfounded.

"How did I know about your new strike?" she asked him, reading his thoughts. "Because Mr. Tito here told me that some of his friends had gone down to work in your mine and had not come up again.

"I immediately suspected that what you were doing was running a secret shift down in the Bluebell. I've been involved in gold mining for many years, as you know. I have heard of such methods before, but I have never known anyone who used them."

"What is this thing, this secret shift?" Josip asked Jessie.

Without taking her eyes off Willoughby, she answered,

"On occasion, when a rich vein of ore is discovered, a mine owner will try his best to keep the news quiet."

But why do such a thing?" Josip asked. "You find gold, you shout with joy, not shut mouth about it."

"Mr. Tito, it can be very profitable if you keep your mouth shut about it, can't it be, Mr. Willoughby?"

"I don't know what you're talking about. What's more, I don't want to know. Get out, both of you."

Jessie ignored the command. "I checked with the Mining Exchange. I learned there that you've been buying up all of your stock that has been offered for sale recently. That convinced me that my suspicions about your having established a secret shift in the Bluebell were probably correct. Just now, when I heard you talking to your manager, I was sure I was right. Your own words indicted you, Mr. Willoughby."

"The way I run my mine is no business of yours. Now, get out or I'll have you thrown out."

"I'll get out," Jessie said quietly. "But first I want to tell you something. If you don't release the men you've been keeping in the mine and release them immediately, I am going to notify contacts I have on the mining exchanges in San Francisco, New York, and Chicago. I will tell them what you are doing and ask them to advise their customers who hold Bluebell shares not to sell them at this time."

Willoughby's lips twitched. He remained silent for a moment and then, "Frazier, go to the hoisting works. Have the Bohunks brought up."

When Frazier had left the office, Jessie said, "There was another reason I wanted to talk to you today, Mr. Willoughby. A reason that preceded my discovery of your secret shift. I wanted to tell you that I intend to negotiate with the strikers, and I've initiated efforts to get other owners to do the same. I wanted to ask you if you would also agree to negotiate."

"I will not. They can rot in hell before I'll give in to them."

"May I point out that you would be doing yourself a favor if you did agree to negotiate. You would be helping to end the strike which has caused all of us grief and is likely to cause us more if my suspicions are correct."

"I will not suffer any grief," Willoughby declared haughtily. "The army will see to that."

"The army?"

"You didn't know?" Willoughby smiled sourly. "I telegraphed the governor. I told him about the strikers derailing a train bringing replacement workers to our mines. I asked him to send a contingent of the state militia here to keep the peace. He has done so. General Sherman Bell, with one thousand troops under his command, arrived here yesterday afternoon and has set up camp north of town. If the strikers cause any more disturbances—even a slight one—they will be imprisoned in the stockade the troops began building when they arrived."

"I can't believe you'd do a thing like that!" an incredulous Jessie exclaimed. "Why use force against the strikers when you could solve the problem—help solve it—simply by sitting down and negotiating?"

"You kick a vicious cur," Willoughby retorted. "You whip a recalcitrant mule. Force is the only thing such dumb brutes understand. Such, I believe is the case with the rabble roused by Dan Calhoun. The army will use force to keep them from causing any more trouble in Cripple Creek."

Jessie, exasperated with what she considered to be Willoughby's stupidity in sending for the militia—or perhaps, she thought, it was a kind of sadism that had motivated him—turned and left the office without another word.

Outside, Josip said, "I am glad my friends will be let out of the mine. But I do not understand this business at all. Why is it bad that Mr. Willoughby buy stock that is for sale? Stock in his own mine? To have shares of business, this is good, no?"

"No. Not in this case. You see, Mr. Tito, what Willoughby has been doing is keeping his new gold strike a secret so that he can make more money than usual in such an event.

"When the gold was first found, he made a deal with your friends to work the vein in secret. To keep them from telling anyone about it, he has kept them down in the mine as part of that deal until such time as he could accomplish what he had in mind."

"Which was?"

"He bought up every share of Bluebell stock he could get his hands on. Why? Because, once he let it be known that a new source of gold had been found in the Bluebell, the mine's per-share price would rise sharply in value."

"Yes, that I understand."

"Then you can also understand that Willoughby, in buying up Bluebell shares, will stand to make an immense profit once the stock does rise upon his release of the news about the gold find."

"Ah, so that is what he does. A sly fox is that Mr. Willoughby. A rich and getting richer soon sly fox."

Jessie thought Josip's words fit Willoughby perfectly. So did a few choice ones she was thinking of but would not say aloud.

"I say thanks to you, miss, for helping my friends. I owe you much."

"You owe me nothing, Mr. Tito. I was glad to be of help."

Josip doffed his hat and bowed to Jessie. "I go now to hoisting works to wait for my friends. I tell them what you do for them. I know they will say thanks to you, too."

Chapter 8

"You were right when you said Horace Willoughby has more crooked cards up his sleeve than any Mississippi riverboat gambler," Jessie told Ki as they breakfasted together early the next morning. "Can you bring yourself to believe that the man is not content with the discovery of a new vein of gold in his mine—that he has to buy up as much of the outstanding stock in his mine as he can get his hands on to maximize his profits? That's not capitalism at work; it's plain greed, in my opinion."

"I have to agree with you, but I also have to say I'm not really all that surprised to hear about the secret shift Willoughby set up to keep the news of the discovery secret until such time as it suited him to reveal it. After all, I told you about the way he was bilking shareholders in that other mine of his."

"His assessment mine."

Ki nodded and forked a crisp piece of salt pork into his

mouth. "The man's a first-class villain in my book, no two ways around it."

"As such he can cause a lot of people a lot of trouble."

"Him and his man, Buster, can."

"I'm worried about Mr. Tippett and his wife," Jessie said after taking a sip of coffee. "Willoughby, as I told you yesterday, has made veiled threats in an attempt to obtain their land."

"He may be bluffing."

"But he may not be."

"Tippett struck me, when I saw him with Calhoun when the strikers were blocking the entrance to the Empire, as a man who can take care of himself."

"I hope so." Jessie emptied her coffee cup. "The thing that disturbs me most about this whole business is that it can be so easily averted. It's just a matter of both sides sitting down together and looking for ways to iron out our differences. But Willoughby is dead set against such an approach."

"Maybe he'll find himself standing alone before very long. You've talked to Cornelius Vandam, and he's agreed to try to get some of the other mine owners to see things your way. If he does and they do—even if only one or two of them do—it might just be enough to isolate Willoughby and any other holdouts."

"I'm not so sure about that. Dan told me none of the strikers will go back to work in any of the mines until such time as all the owners have come to terms with them."

"Bullheaded fellow, isn't he?"

"I can see why he takes the position he does. If some of the strikers go back to work in a mine or two, that leaves the others out in the cold. He's right in wanting to maintain a united front against the mine owners."

"You sound like you're on his side now."

"I'm not. It's just that, as I said, I can understand his

132

position, and I confess, were I in his place, I'd probably do the very same thing."

"Calhoun had better keep his men—and himself—on a tight rein," Ki mused. "If he doesn't the army will step in, and then we're liable to see some real fireworks."

"As I told you, when Willoughby said he'd petitioned the governor to send the state militia here, I was stunned. I think that's carrying things much too far."

"It's not a move likely to smooth the strikers' ruffled feathers. Force breeds force, in my experience. One side attacks, and then the other side feels compelled to make an even stronger stand if for no other reason than to save face."

"I'd like to talk to the commander of the militia," Jessie said, a worried look on her face. "I want to know just what his plans are."

"Do you think he'd tell you what they are?"

"I don't see why not. I'm a mine owner. He'll assume I feel the same way about the strike and the strikers as Willoughby does, so I think he'll be glad to talk to me."

"When do you want to drive out and have a talk with him?"

"This morning. As soon as we're finished here, if that's all right with you. I don't want to waste any time because I have the uneasy feeling I've got to plug a few holes here and there before the flood waters start flowing through them and we all drown."

"It's a wonder there's anyone left in the army to protect the rest of the state," Ki marveled as he and Jessie drove through Paupers' Patch and then into the army camp. They drove between two neat rows of tents beyond which were several other rows. Around them, the air was filled with the sound of hammers and saws hard at work in the hands of soldiers.

133

Ki slowed the carriage and asked one of them where he could find General Bell.

"Right down at the end of this here row, sir," the soldier responded cheerfully. "It's on your right when you get there."

"Thank you." Ki drove on and drew rein when he reached the tent on the right at the end of the long row. He stepped down to the ground and joined Jessie, who was heading for the open tent flap through which could be seen a uniformed man seated at a camp table as he pored over a large map spread out before him.

"General Sherman Bell?"

The man looked up at Jessie. "Yes, I'm General Bell. Who are you?"

"I'm Jessica Starbuck. I own the Empire Gold Mine in Cripple Creek."

General Bell rose and rounded his camp table. "I'm pleased to make your acquaintance. Forgive me for not having greeted you more cordially. I was momentarily taken aback at the sight of a woman here in my camp. What can I do for you? Other than to assure you that we will soon have things under our firm control so that there is no need for you to fret on that score?"

"I *am* fretting, General. I—"

"I assure you there is nothing for you to worry about. The stockade we're building is almost finished. We have stationed guards at each of the mines that have been struck. We are making plans to supply a military escort to the strikebreakers as they report for work at the mines in an effort to avoid any clashes with the miners they have replaced."

"Your men, I take it, will be armed?" Jessie asked.

General Bell looked at her as if she were simple. "Of course they will be."

"Do they have orders to shoot?" Ki inquired.

General Bell looked at him as if he were an intruder.

"This is a friend of mine, General. His name is Ki."

"I see. Well, to reply to your question, sir, my men have orders to shoot if they must in order to defend themselves."

"How do they decide if they need to defend themselves?" Ki asked.

"Their commanders will evaluate each situation as it arises and give the order to fire if, in their judgment, such an order is warranted. I have only seasoned troops with me, so you needn't be alarmed. There will be no unnecessary engagements."

"I don't want to see *any* engagements, General, of any kind," Jessie said hotly.

"I don't understand. You said, did you not, that you are a mine owner?"

"I did, yes, but I for one am against the use of military force in a strike situation such as the one we are presently facing. I came here to ask you to keep your troops in camp and not to involve yourself in any contact with either the strikers or the men who have replaced them."

"Surely you realize that I cannot accede to your wishes, however much I might wish to do so. I have my orders from the governor. I would be derelict in my duty were I not to obey them to the letter."

"What exactly are your orders, General?" Ki asked.

"To smash this anarchistic federation you've got festering here!" General Bell stormed. "To stamp it out, to crush it completely!"

"You intend to imprison the strikers in your stockade?" Jessie inquired, although she was sure she knew the answer to the question.

"The strikers and their sympathizers as well," General Bell replied, his eyes boring into Jessie's.

"I suggest to you, General," she said, "that you might find yourself in violation of the Constitution of the United

States if you imprison people without due process."

"Due process be damned!" General Bell exclaimed, losing his temper, pounding a fist on his camp table and overturning it. "I will not have a rabid bunch of anarchists running around loose and doing harm everywhere and in every way they can. You talk to me of the Constitution, Miss Starbuck. Well, I suggest to you that you would do well to go instead to the men—led, I'm told, by one Dan Calhoun—and talk to those bomb-throwing anarchists about due process and the like!"

"I urge you to reconsider your position, General Bell," Jessie said as calmly as she could.

"There is nothing to reconsider. I have a job to do and I intend to do it."

Jessie, working hard at controlling her temper, which was about to flare up at any moment, turned and left General Bell's tent. As she made her way back to the carriage with Ki, she could hear General Bell cursing behind her as he savagely kicked the camp table he had upset, reducing it to kindling.

She chose to drive on the return trip to town because she wanted to work off some of her anger through physical effort.

"That man obviously relishes his job," she muttered, giving her horse free rein. "I'm convinced General Bell actually enjoys the assignment he's been given."

"He's not what you could call a man of even temperament," Ki observed.

"He's a man with a mission. Such men can be dangerous."

"Depending upon the nature of their mission."

"I think he sees the one he's been given as a way to save the law-abiding world from those he insists on labeling 'anarchists.' That's ludicrous. Dan Calhoun is no more an anarchist than I am or you are."

136

"To give the devil his due, the general did say he had ordered his subordinates not to fire unless they had to in self-defense."

"Mere words," Jessie remarked disdainfully. "I wouldn't be the least bit surprised if the militia under our zealous General Bell would fire in self-defense at a cow that came at them when all the poor beast wanted was the relief afforded by a milking."

"There's a saying—"

Jessie gave Ki a sidelong glance. "Not another one of your made-to-order Japanese proverbs, I hope."

Ki smiled. "No, this one's American. Or maybe British, I'm not sure. It goes like this: 'The proof of the pudding is in the eating.'"

"Which means what in this particular situation?"

"That we'll have to wait and see if General Bell's deeds match his words."

"That prospect doesn't make me feel one whit more comfortable."

"There's smoke up ahead," Ki observed as they entered Paupers' Patch. "Maybe somebody's chimney's on fire."

"Fire!" a man shouted, echoing Ki's last word as he darted in front of the carriage, forcing Jessie to draw rein so sharply that the bit cut into the horse's lips.

"That fool!" she muttered, unnerved. "He could have gotten himself killed running in front of us so recklessly." Then, as smoke billowed black against the sky, she frowned.

"What's the matter?" Ki asked her.

"Mr. Tippett's house is over that way where the smoke is, as I recall."

"He's the fellow Calhoun took you to visit, isn't he?"

"Yes. Let's drive over there and see what's burning."

"Better leave the carriage here. There's a crowd headed

that way. We'll get bogged down for sure if we try to drive in that direction."

Jessie put on the brake, and then she and Ki made their way on foot, together with many other people, toward the site of the fire.

"It's the Tippetts' house!" a shocked Jessie exclaimed moments later when the burning building came into view.

"Are there any souls inside?" a frightened woman cried in alarm to no one in particular. "Oh, 'tis a terrible thing, 'tis fire."

"Send for the fire engine!" someone shouted, and another man on the fringe of the growing crowd responded with, "Denny Kildare has sent his youngest to fetch the engine. Little Brian's fleet of foot. The firemen'll be here in no time flat."

"Where are they?" an anxious Jessie asked several minutes later when no firemen had appeared on the scene. "The fire is spreading so fast that the firemen will be of no use if they don't get here soon."

In the distance a church bell began to ring.

"That must be the signal that there's a fire," Ki speculated, turning and peering up and down the street, where no firemen or fire engine was as yet visible.

"Watch where you walk!" a man near Jessie boomed in anger as someone came hurtling through the crowd. "You near knocked me down, you did!"

"It's Mr. Tippett," Jessie said as he emerged from the crowd.

"Oh, my Lord a'mercy!" he wailed when he saw the flames sprouting from his house, and Dan Calhoun appeared at his side.

"May!" Tippett screamed, both hands cupped around his mouth in order to make himself heard over the increasing roar of the fire. *"May, where are you?"*

Jessie and Ki hurried over to him.

"Is your wife inside the house, Mr. Tippett?" Jessie asked.

Tippett seemed not to have heard her. He stood staring at the blaze, his mouth working, his eyes watering either from tears or because of the stinging smoke that a wayward wind suddenly sent flowing downward to the ground in great black clouds.

Calhoun repeated Jessie's question.

"Dan, it's not sure I am," Tippett answered. "She was here when I left to meet you. She'd not had breakfast. She'd been having the morning sickness something terrible and said she couldn't keep so much as a drop of water down."

"Might she have gone to a neighbor's house?" Calhoun asked.

"Or to visit a friend?" Jessie added.

"I don't think so," Tippett responded to both questions. "She was feeling too poorly for that. *May!*" he cried again.

But his anguished cry was lost in the happy hurrahs of the crowd as a team of firemen came racing down the street pulling their fire engine.

"Make way!" one of them bellowed, and another chimed in with, "Stand back everybody!"

The crowd held its ground until Calhoun and Ki, working jointly and silently, moved them back to make room for the firemen and their engine. Both men then joined the firemen and proceeded to help man the pumps.

Water squirted onto the fire from the engine.

Ki, pumping as hard and as fast as he could, muttered to Calhoun on his right, "This thing's not fit for much more than watering somebody's flower garden. The stream of water doesn't go more than forty feet, and it's a thin stream, too."

Calhoun, grim-faced, pumped on, his eyes on the house and the flames that were swiftly devouring it.

"Shoot that water up to damp down the roof!" one of the firemen, who seemed to be in charge, ordered.

Up went the water as down fell a rain of hot ash and cinders.

"May's surely not inside, Mr. Tippett," Jessie said, trying to reassure the man. "She would have had time to get out before the fire got this bad had she been in there."

"She said she might go back to bed," a numb Tippett said. "She's a heavy sleeper, May is."

Jessie tried to think of something else to say, something that might comfort Tippett. But nothing came to her. She didn't know if May Tippett was or was not inside the house. She put an arm around Tippett's shaking shoulders.

She had no sooner done so when Tippett broke away from her and went running toward the house.

Jessie turned and saw May Tippett framed in a ground floor window where she stood, her trembling hands spreading the curtains that were already ablaze, as were her clothes and her hair.

"May!" Tippett screamed as he reached the house. He kicked the front door open and ran inside before anyone could stop him.

A woman in the crowd screamed.

A fireman cursed.

Jessie's hands flew up to cover her mouth. She moaned at the sight of Tippett as he appeared at the door with May cradled in his arms, both of them now burning, the flames that had been consuming May having spread to her husband like some loathsome and highly contagious disease.

Tippett staggered forward a few steps. His face began to char. A terrible sound, a nonhuman sound, escaped his lips. He staggered forward another step . . .

The front wall of the house collapsed, burying him and May and the unborn child May had been carrying.

A collective cry went up from the crowd, a wordless wail of despair that was mixed with horror.

"Glory be to God!" an awed man near Jessie murmured as he crossed himself while continuing to stare at the flames which were too much of a match for the many gallons of water being pumped upon them.

Jessie turned her back to the fire as if to deny its power by making it invisible. But she could feel its penetrating heat on her back. Tears filled her eyes.

Ki, seeing her distress, commandeered another man to work his position on the pump, and then left it to come to her side.

She turned, a stricken expression on her face. Then, as a sound like a shot from a cannon sounded, she started and turned in time to see the last of the Tippett house's timbers, most charred and some still blazing, fall to the ground.

The collapsing house sent a bright cloud of embers skyward, which then began to fall upon the spectators. Men and women slapped them away, crying out in pain as their hands touched the tiny living coals. They hurriedly backed away, as did Ki, who led Jessie to a spot far enough from the inferno to be free of any wayward sparks.

A stunned Calhoun joined them. He stood there shaking his head as he gazed at the pyre that had once been a home. "We were at a strikers' meeting, Billy and I," he said softly. "It had been a good meeting, one which gave us all a lot of hope that the strike could eventually be settled. On our way back here, Billy was in good spirits. He talked of the future. Of May's baby that was on its way. He said he was hoping for a son, but that a daughter would be a delight as well."

Staring at the dying fire amid which stood a smoke-blackened stone chimney, Jessie said, "I wonder how the fire started." She carefully avoided looking at the pile of

141

rubble beneath which Billy and May Tippett's burned bodies lay.

"It could have started in any number of ways," Calhoun declared. "A log burning in the fireplace could have collapsed, and an ember might have been thrown out onto the wooden floor beyond the stone flags of the hearth."

"There was no smoke coming from the chimney when we arrived," Ki stated.

"May might have dropped a lighted lamp," Calhoun suggested.

"It's hardly likely that she would have needed a lighted lamp in broad daylight," Ki said.

"A match—she might have struck a match for some reason—and dropped it," Calhoun proposed.

"Struck a match for what reason?" Ki asked.

"I don't know. Any reason at all."

Ki merely stared at Calhoun.

Jessie, knowing her friend, said, "You think the fire wasn't an accident."

"I think," Ki said, "that it might not have been an accident."

"You mean you think it was deliberately set," Jessie said, pressing her point.

"It very well might have been. There was no fire in the hearth. It's unlikely that May would have needed to light a lamp."

"But who—" Jessie began and then fell silent. She looked from Ki to Calhoun, who said, "Willoughby."

"Maybe," Ki said tentatively.

"Buster," Jessie said.

"Maybe," Ki repeated. Then he added in a lower tone, "I'd like to try to find out how the fire started—or who started it. To that end, I think I'll mosey around the neighborhood when things start to settle down. Ask a few questions. Maybe somebody saw something suspicious before the fire started. Or *someone* suspicious. I'll drive you back to the hotel, Jessie, and then come back here and see what, if anything, I can find out."

"You needn't drive me back, Ki."

"You're sure you're all right?"

"Well, no, I'm not. But I can manage. You go ahead and ask your questions. I'll see you later at the hotel."

Ki nodded and then made his way toward the house that flanked the Tippett house on the left.

"Can I give you a ride back to town?" Jessie asked Calhoun.

He gave her a wry smile. "Wouldn't that be something for the townspeople to talk about? Dan Calhoun, leader of the Cripple Creek miners' strike, riding in a carriage with none other than Miss Jessica Starbuck, owner of the Empire Mine. I tell you, a sight like that would be enough to keep tongues wagging for the next month of Sundays at least."

Jessie, in no mood for levity, said, "Is your answer yes or no?"

"It's yes."

"Then let's go. I can't wait to get out of here."

Calhoun, as he followed her to her carriage, asked if she wanted him to drive.

"Would you mind? Despite what I told Ki, I'm feeling a little shaky."

"That's no wonder after what we all just witnessed. It's enough to make anyone shaky if not downright scared."

As they drove away from Paupers' Patch, Jessie gave Calhoun a sidelong glance and said, "You think the fire was set, don't you?"

"I tried to find reasons which would explain how it might have started. But you heard Ki find the flaws in all of them. Yes, I think now—and even thought then, I suppose—that someone might have torched the Tippett house."

Jessie shuddered. "I know what you mean about how such a thing could frighten people. It certainly frightens me—the thought that someone would dare to do such a thing."

"Someone?"

When Jessie said nothing, Calhoun continued, "When word of the fire spreads, there are going to be some hotheads among my men if they come to the same tentative conclusion that we have reached."

"You have an obligation to remind them that there is—at least at this juncture—no proof that the fire was anything other than an accident."

"You're right about that. But there are more than a few men among the strikers who get some of their exercise from jumping to conclusions in cases like this. Unproven conclusions, that is."

"It worries me, hearing you say that."

"As well it should."

As they pulled up in front of the hotel, Jessie asked, "What are we going to do about this situation, Mr. Calhoun?"

"You mean about the fire and what trouble might rise up out of its ashes?"

"Yes."

"I'd like to discuss that issue with you at greater length —if you'll consent to call me Dan and permit me to call you Jessica, since we're long past the point of such formalities as 'Miss' this and 'Mr.' that."

"Most people call me Jessie—Dan."

Calhoun, smiling broadly, helped Jessie down from the carriage.

"Would you like to come up to my room?" Jessie had no sooner asked the question than she wondered if the expres-

144

sion on her face betrayed what she was thinking about Dan Calhoun and the invitation she had just tendered him.

He readily accepted her invitation, and when they were in Jessie's room with the door closed behind them, he said with mock solemnity, "My men might call my being here with you like this consorting with the enemy."

"I hope we aren't enemies any longer, Mr.—Dan."

"So do I most fervently hope."

Jessie sat down on a chair near the door. Calhoun chose one near the window opposite her.

To Jessie, the bed seemed to dominate the room. She scrupulously avoided looking at it.

An awkward silence seemed to thunder in the room.

Calhoun finally broke it by clearing his throat and saying, "I wish different circumstances had brought us together, Jessie."

"We're here to talk about—"

Calhoun rose, quickly crossed the room, and brought Jessie to her feet. "I want to talk about you. How beautiful you are. How desirable you are."

She didn't struggle against him. It was as if she had known what was coming and been both ready and eager for it. Her body melded against Calhoun's, and his kiss, when it came, was sweet.

But she felt compelled to protest despite her desire for this handsome and very virile man in whose arms she wanted to remain. "After what just happened to the Tippetts—Dan, we can't. We mustn't."

His lips nuzzled her neck. "Jessie, we can. That was Death. This—we—are Life."

Jessie tried and failed to muster a further protest. She let herself surrender to Calhoun's lips and his hot arousing hands, to the lust for him that was now seething so strongly within her.

145

Then, recovering herself somewhat, she began to undress.

Taking his cue from her, Calhoun began to do the same.

Jessie lay down upon the bed and held up her arms to him. He sank down upon her with a sigh and an exhalation of breath that was hot upon her cheek.

As he covered her body with his, he nudged her legs apart with his own.

Fully aroused now, his erection throbbed and spasmed as he thrust into her.

She clutched him to her, holding him as if she never intended to let him go. Her hands gripped his buttocks, and she tried to pull him deeper into her. She moaned as he slammed into her.

Suddenly Calhoun tensed. A low cry escaped his lips as he exploded within Jessie.

A moment later she, too, reached a climax.

For a few minutes their sweating, heaving bodies lay next to each other. He whispered erotic words of desire in her ear, which soon led to a second, even more exciting, climax.

★

Chapter 9

Jessie squirmed in the bed beside Calhoun. She stretched, luxuriating in the warmth of his body next to hers and the memory of their lovemaking that had so stirred her passions. She turned on her side and playfully tapped her fingers on his chest.

"Mmmmm" was his response as he lay on his back with his eyes closed, a faint smile on his face.

Jessie propped herself up with one hand, leaned over, and kissed him on the lips. "You were concerned about what people would say if they saw us riding together in my carriage," she murmured. Then, teasingly, "What do you suppose they'd say if they could see us now?"

Calhoun opened his eyes. His face assumed an expression of mock horror—eyes wide, lips twisted in a grimace. "I would be deposed as the leader of the strikers. I might even be tarred and feathered and run out of town on a rail."

"I promise not to tell if you won't."

"I definitely won't tell. It would mean the ruin of my

hard-earned reputation as a fighter against the rich and powerful interests that would exploit the lowly working man."

"This is what the sides we represent should be doing."

"You mean to say the strikers and the mine owners should be in bed with one another?"

"In a sense, yes. But I didn't mean what I said in a literal sense. I meant that both sides should be getting together and trying to settle the strike in an amicable manner."

"Well, what we've been doing," Calhoun said, his grin widening, "was certainly amicable enough."

"Oh, you know what I mean!"

Sobering, Calhoun nodded. "I do and I agree with you. When we first met at the train derailment, I never in a million years thought I would hear myself saying I agreed with you on anything, but look—the world has turned and here we are."

"I'm glad. Aren't you?"

"I am."

"I spoke to Cornelius Vandam yesterday. He agreed to try to persuade other mine owners to negotiate with your men. I'll have to go and see him to find out what, if anything, he was able to accomplish in that regard."

"That's progress of a sort. Important progress."

"Well, yes, but don't count your chickens before they're hatched. Cornelius told me that some of the other owners have good reasons not to go against Willoughby."

"Willoughby!" Calhoun spat the word into the room. "If he were not in the picture, I'll bet my bottom dollar this strike would have been over long ago. In fact, it might not have happened in the first place without Willoughby's recalcitrant stand against us. The other owners might have made concessions—"

"And the miners might have made concessions?"

148

"Well—"

"Well?"

"Yes, the miners might have made concessions. The whole affair might have turned out to be a tempest in a teapot."

"Instead of a potential war between the army and a group of civilians."

Calhoun swore under his breath. "When I found out that the militia had been sent here—that was the straw that just about broke this camel's back!" he exclaimed heatedly. "Can you imagine anything more unnecessary than Willoughby's petitioning the governor to send in troops to try to crush the strike by armed—and possibly deadly—force?"

"You call Willoughby's move unnecessary. I doubt that he gave much thought to whether or not it was necessary. I suspect that he simply chose that option as one more in his arsenal, any one of which by itself might help him attain his goal."

"Which is to grind the men working in the mines down into the dirt and to treat them like that very dirt for the rest of their downtrodden lives!"

A muted roar suddenly invaded the room. It was quickly followed by a series of lesser rumbles.

"What was that?" a startled Jessie asked, sitting up in bed.

Calhoun sprang from the bed and went to the window. Drawing aside the curtain, he peered out.

"Dan?"

"To answer your question, I'd say those were explosions we just heard."

"Where?"

"There's some smoke rising west of town."

"Willoughby's Bluebell Mine is over in that direction."

"I'm going to see what happened." Calhoun left the

149

window and proceeded to dress as fast as he could.

"I'm going with you." Jessie got out of bed, and she, too, began to dress, worry etching lines on her usually smooth forehead.

As Jessie and Calhoun arrived at the Bluebell Mine in her carriage, they found the place the center of a mob scene.

Strikers milled about, most of them shouting loud and often obscene denunciations of Horace Willoughby. A crowd of onlookers had gathered nearby, drawn to the spot, as Jessie and Calhoun had been, by the sound of the explosions. Many of them shouted excited words of encouragement to the strikers. In and out among the two groups of people ran several braying mules which had somehow been released or had broken out of the enclosure where they were corralled when not hauling ore carts.

"Good God, it's a madhouse!" Calhoun declared as he jumped down from the carriage.

Jessie joined him on the ground. Both of them stood staring at the melee before them.

"They're going to—" Jessie began, but she never got to finish whatever it was she had been about to say because the ear-splitting sound of another explosion tore through the air as the Bluebell's shaft house was blown to bits.

Calhoun took her in his arms to shield her from the flying debris that the explosion had sent swirling through the air. He covered her body with his own, his back to the site of the explosion, as broken boards went sailing through the air, one of them striking him a sharp blow on the left shoulder.

"We've went and done it, Dan!" a gleeful striker shouted.

Calhoun glanced over his shoulder at the man. "Done what, have you?"

"We planted explosives in the shaft house and ran a

connecting wire to the woods over there, and when we pushed the button, the place went sky-high, it damn well did!"

"You could have killed somebody—maybe a whole lot of somebodies, you damned fool!" Calhoun shouted at the striking miner, who was wearing a smile as big as a half-moon.

"None of *us* was inside the place," the man responded.

"Whatever possessed you to do such a dangerous thing?" Jessie demanded to know.

"We heard all about what Willoughby did to Billy and May Tippett and the bairn she was bearing."

"You know for a fact that Willoughby was responsible for the Tippett fire?" Calhoun asked.

"Aye, that's what everybody's been saying, Dan."

"That's not proof, man!" Calhoun bellowed. "The fact that everybody's saying something doesn't mean—"

His next words were drowned out by another violent explosion. This one sent the Bluebell's boiler shooting up into the air in an uncountable number of pieces.

Steam also shot up from broken pipes to be whipped away by the rising wind.

"Lookee there, Dan!" the gleeful striker called out, pointing to a nearby bluff.

"What the hell—" Calhoun breathed when he saw the makeshift catapult manned by strikers on top of the bluff.

Even as he and Jessie watched, its huge wooden arm was released to send a number of dynamite-filled beer bottles hurtling through the air toward the mine's stamp mill.

They missed their target, but as they struck and exploded on the roof of the nearby business office, they nearly demolished the building.

"Here you go, Danny boy!" the striker exclaimed, pulling from his pocket a deadly missile and handing it to Calhoun—a missile consisting of five sticks of dynamite fitted with percussion caps, all bound together with a piece of wire. "You can come close to taking out the whole shebang with that there," the man exulted.

"I don't want the damned thing," Calhoun snarled. "And I don't want to see you using it, either," he added, handing it back.

"But, Danny, my boy—"

The striker's words fell on empty air because Calhoun had gone racing toward a loaded ore cart that sat on a track near the mine.

Jessie's fists clenched with tension as she watched him go. She gave a little cry as more dynamite-filled beer bottles came flying through the air to land at the edge of the crowd of strikers, where they sent up dark clouds of dust and some sparks.

"Stop it!"

Calhoun's shouted command was a kind of explosion of its own. He stood atop the ore cart now, his arms raised to get the attention of the men who were attacking the Bluebell Mine.

"Stop it!" he repeated, less loudly as a hush fell on the gathered crowd. "This is not the way to get what we want. Not by destroying property. What would you men do? Destroy the Bluebell, where some of you worked and where, I *presume*, you hope someday to return to work? That way lies madness, men!"

"We mean to show Willoughby he can't burn down a man's house and kill him and his wife in the process, Dan!" shouted an obviously irate striker.

"You don't know that Willoughby was responsible for that fire!" Calhoun shouted back.

"We don't want to hear no more of your fine words, Dan Calhoun!" another striker yelled. "We seen who you come here with. That Starbuck woman is who we seen you come here with. Which makes more than me wonder what

152

you're up to. What is it you're out to get for your own self by consorting with one of them that's our enemy?"

"Miss Starbuck and I have been on the verge of coming to terms over wages and working conditions in her mine for some time now. We—"

Jessie didn't hear the rest of what Calhoun had to say because Ki suddenly appeared at her side and said, "It looks like they mean to blow the whole place up."

"They already did blow up the shaft house and the boiler."

"What started this ruckus, do you know?"

"The strikers are blaming Willoughby for the fire that killed the Tippetts and destroyed their home. They're here for revenge."

"They know Willoughby was behind the fire, do they?"

"No, that's what's so terrible about this. They don't know. They have no proof of the charges they're making. But they seem hell-bent on destroying the Bluebell anyway. They seem to think they don't *need* proof."

"Vigilante justice."

"Were you able to find out anything in Paupers' Patch?"

Ki shook his head. "No one saw anything or anyone suspicious—or so they all say. But they also all say they firmly believe Willoughby was behind it. So I guess I shouldn't be surprised at this, although, when I heard the first explosion, I *was* surprised."

"Get down out of there!" one of the strikers yelled at Calhoun, at whom he was pointing a rigid finger. "You're not fit to lead the strike no more. All you're fit for is to hobnob with the rich and powerful like that Starbuck woman."

Muttering ran through the mob of men, an ominous sound.

"We'll take a voice vote," announced the man who had just called for Calhoun to step down from the ore cart. "Do we want Dan Calhoun representing us in any future bargaining with the mine owners or do we want a new man we can trust? One who won't try to play both sides off against the middle?"

"That's not fair!" Jessie protested. "Dan's not—"

"Voice vote, voice vote!" chanted the men in the crowd.

"So be it," said the man who had just proposed the procedure. "All in favor of Calhoun, say aye!"

"Wait a minute!" Jessie shouldered her way through the crowd until she reached the ore cart on which Calhoun still stood in a defiant posture, his arms folded across his chest. "Help me up there," she said to him, and he did.

"Apparently some of you men know me," she said when she was standing beside Calhoun. "I'm Jessica Starbuck and I own the Empire Mine. I have something I want to say to you all."

"Maybe we don't want to hear what you have to say to us!" a voice in the crowd called out.

Joyless laughter rippled through the crowd.

"You men may have grievances against Miss Starbuck," Calhoun roared, "but I hope to heaven you have the common decency as gentlemen to let her speak her piece. Or have you lost your manners along with your senses and tempers?"

Calhoun's words succeeded in calming the men by shaming them into an uneasy silence.

"I've agreed to sit down and negotiate with Mr. Calhoun about wages and working conditions," Jessie told the crowd. "Now I want you all to understand that that does not mean I agree with every demand you men have made. Neither does it mean that I will give in to every demand you have made. What I will do, though, and on this you have my solemn word, is listen carefully to your proposals and your grievances and then make decisions on what, if any, changes should be made in the way the Empire operates in the future."

"What about the other mines?" someone in the crowd wanted to know. "I don't work at your Empire, so what good is your talking to Calhoun going to do me is what I need to know."

"I have spoken to Mr. Cornelius Vandam, president of the Vandam Mining Company. He is considering taking the same position in regard to the strike that I have taken."

A few weak cheers went up from some of the men listening to Jessie.

She held up a hand for quiet. "Wait. There's more. Mr. Vandam, at my urging, has agreed to speak to other mine owners and to try to persuade them to agree to negotiate with you to put an end to this strike that none of us really wants."

"We want it if it'll get us what's our due!" a man at the front of the crowd shouted up at Jessie.

"Is this the way you think you'll get what you want?" she shot back. "By bombing the Bluebell? By damaging it and running the risk of hurting—maybe killing—someone in the infernal process? Does this make sense to all of you?"

There were a few cries of "Yes!" but, by and large, most of the men remained silent.

Jessie, pressing what she perceived to be her advantage, continued: "There's a better way. It's called negotiations."

"What's Horace Willoughby's way?" someone in the crowd wanted to know.

"Burning us out," someone shouted, "so he can get his hands on our land!"

"I had nothing whatsoever to do with the Tippett fire!"

Jessie looked away from the upturned faces below her to where Willoughby had appeared in his carriage, Buster seated beside him.

A muttering began among the men as they turned to stare at the mine owner.

"You dare to defame me!" he shouted angrily, shaking a fist at the men gathered in front of his mine. "You dare to slander me, to throw mud on my good name!" he spluttered. "I will not have it! Nor will I have you damaging my property as you have been doing. I want you all off this land. *Right now!* That includes you, Miss Starbuck! As far as I am concerned, you are as harmful in your way as are these destructive strikers. Do what you please in your own mining operation, but I will thank you to leave mine *alone!*"

"You're going to lose in the end, Mr. Willoughby!" Jessie cried. "You will have to come to terms with these men sooner or later. We all will. Why not let it be now before there is any more trouble?"

"There will not be any more trouble, Miss Starbuck," Willoughby declared in an oily tone. "What trouble there has been already will be speedily and severely punished."

"What the hell might you be meaning by that remark, Willoughby?" someone shouted.

"You'll all learn soon enough—to your sorrow," he replied with a self-satisfied smirk.

"What do you suppose the old windbag's talking about?" Calhoun asked Jessie.

Before she could reply, General Sherman Bell suddenly appeared leading a large contingent of state militia.

Silence seized the strikers and the people who had joined them at the mine.

Bell marched on, his men following him. Through the silence he marched until he came to the outermost fringe of the crowd, where he proceeded to shout loud orders to his men.

Those orders galvanized the strikers. They began to

shout defiance at the militia, and some of them began to flee from the scene.

The soldiers pursued them.

"You've got no right to be here!" Calhoun yelled at Bell.

The general barely deigned to glance in his direction. He did not deign to answer Calhoun's charge.

But Willoughby did. Standing up in his carriage and still smirking, he called out, "The militia has every right in the world to be here, Calhoun. They have been ordered here by the governor of this sovereign state. I, for one, am glad they are here to remove you and your rabble, who *truly* have no right to be here."

"Take it easy, Dan," Jessie cautioned as Calhoun, his eyes afire, was about to respond to Willoughby. "Don't do anything that might endanger you or your men."

"It looks to me," he muttered, "like we're already in danger. That tin soldier down there's rounding up everybody in sight, damn him!"

Jessie could see that what Calhoun had said was true. The soldiers, all of them with their weapons drawn, were herding strikers and sympathetic members of the crowd into a tight but ever-widening circle. Among them were several women and two small children, one of whom, a girl, had begun to cry as she tugged at her mother's skirt.

A soldier approached the ore cart. "Get down from there, you two," he ordered, gesturing with the barrel of his army Colt.

Calhoun helped Jessie climb down from the cart and then joined her on the ground.

"Take that man into custody at once!" General Bell bellowed, pointing at Calhoun.

As three soldiers responded to their commander's order, Calhoun attacked the first one to approach him, knocking the man down with a powerful right uppercut.

157

Jessie winced as a second soldier struck Calhoun on the back of the head with the butt of his Colt.

Calhoun faltered. His knees began to buckle and he almost went down.

Jessie sprinted to where Ki was standing some distance away. When she reached him, she said, "We've got to do something to help Dan."

"Stay here."

Ignoring Ki's command, Jessie hurried after him as he ran over to where Calhoun and the three militiamen were battling.

By the time he, with Jessie not far behind him, reached Calhoun, the man was down on both knees and being beaten by all three of the soldiers with their gun barrels, fists, and feet.

Ki grabbed one of the soldiers just as the man was about to deliver a savage kick to Calhoun's ribs. He turned him around and, practicing the "hidden hand" technique he had learned during his study of the ancient art of *jujutsu*, he struck a forceful blow called a *chen chih*, or Needle Finger. The soldier, struck just below the right ear at the location of the vagus nerve, stiffened, blinked, and then fell unconscious to the ground.

"What the hell?" a second soldier exclaimed as he saw his companion go down. He left off clubbing a now badly bloodied Calhoun to turn on Ki. He raised his revolver, his finger on its trigger.

Jessie darted forward. Crouching, she came in under the soldier's upraised arm. Her left arm deftly knocked aside the soldier's gunhand while her right streaked out to deliver a devastating blow, a *te ch'ang chuan*, to the man's midsection, a maneuver she had been taught by Ki.

The soldier gasped, doubled over, and dropped his weapon.

Ki delivered the coup de grace with a stiff right hand that landed on the back of the man's neck.

The third soldier voluntarily dropped his weapon. Holding up his hands in front of him and shaking his head from side to side, he began to back away from the fray.

Ki lunged at him. His feint had the desired effect. The soldier turned and fled.

Jessie and Ki helped Calhoun to his feet.

"I feel like I've been hit by a train," Calhoun muttered as he tried to wipe the blood from his forehead which was dripping into his eyes and clouding his vision.

"Stand aside, Miss Starbuck!"

Jessie glanced over her shoulder to find General Bell himself, flanked by Willoughby and Buster, standing there with a gun leveled at Calhoun.

Fury boiled within her at the sight of the three men. "I will not stand aside," she declared. "This man has been badly hurt by your soldiers, General, and my friend, Ki, and I intend to help him."

"You'll do no such thing," Willoughby snapped. "That man is going to the stockade along with all the others of his ilk."

"Oh, no, he's not!" Jessie insisted. "He needs medical care, not confinement."

"He needs to be taught a lesson," Willoughby declared angrily. "Well, General, don't just stand there. Take the bastard into custody."

General Bell raised a hand and summoned a soldier who was passing by and nursing a bloody head wound with a soiled handkerchief.

"Sir?" said the man, snapping to attention and saluting.

"Take this man to the stockade with the rest of the people we've rounded up."

"Yes, sir." The soldier dropped his handkerchief and drew his revolver. "This way," he barked at Calhoun.

"It's all right, Jessie," Calhoun said softly, touching her arm. "I'll be out in due time, and when I am I intend to redouble my efforts to win this struggle we're engaged in."

"I fully intend to help Mr. Calhoun do just that," Jessie surprised herself by saying as she addressed both General Bell and Horace Willoughby. "I plan first to telegraph the governor, who is, by the way, an old friend of the Starbuck family. I plan to tell him that I think what is being done here is neither necessary nor legal, and I plan to ask him to withdraw the troops. Then I plan to try my very best to convince the other mine owners, with the single exception of Mr. Willoughby, to meet with Mr. Calhoun in a sincere effort to end this strike. Then—"

"Miss Starbuck," Willoughby interrupted, "you will rue the day you first took sides with the anarchists. I warn you—you will regret the position you've taken here today against the rest of the mine owners, and you will regret it deeply."

"Is that a threat, Mr. Willoughby?"

"I am not in the habit of making threats. I *am*, however, in the habit of making promises when I know I can keep those promises."

The soldier marched Calhoun away at gunpoint.

The pair had not gone far when Calhoun looked back over his shoulder and gave Jessie a reassuring smile that seemed to say she was not to worry, he would be fine.

She wasn't so sure about that. Turning to General Bell, she said evenly, "I am going into town now, General, and I am going to hire the best lawyer I can find there to represent Dan Calhoun and the other people you have just taken into custody. He will challenge your authority to act as you have, but first I intend to direct him to obtain from the court writs of habeas corpus which will lead to the prompt release of the people you have imprisoned in your stockade."

"Habeas corpus, is it?" General Bell responded quickly, arching an eyebrow as he stared with unmistakable disdain at Jessie. "Since we seem to be showing off our knowledge of the Latin language today, let me inform you, Miss Starbuck, that you may obtain all the writs of habeas corpus you want. I just may give your lawyer—and anybody else who makes the bad mistake of getting in my militia's way —*postmortems*! How do you like that Latin, Miss Starbuck?"

Jessie didn't like it at all, but she made no retort. She merely stood her ground watching General Bell, Willoughby, and Buster stride away.

When they had gone, she spoke to Ki. As soon as we get back to town, I'll wire the governor about what happened here today and ask him to withdraw the militia or at least forbid the imprisoning of anyone. Then I intend to hire a lawyer to help free the people already taken into custody. In the meantime, to save precious time, I wonder if you would do something for me."

"Name it, I'll do it."

"Would you go to see Cornelius Vandam and ask him if he has had any luck in getting any of the other mine owners to agree to negotiate and end the strike? If he has failed to do so, I will meet personally with each of them and try to persuade them to talk to Dan."

"Where will I find this Vandam fellow?"

Jessie gave Ki the address of the Vandam Mining Company's office and then said, "I'll see you later back at the hotel."

★

Chapter 10

"I'm pleased to make your acquaintance, Ki," Cornelius Vandam said as he welcomed Ki to his office. "Any friend of Jessie Starbuck's is a friend of mine." He seated himself behind his desk and waved Ki into a chair beside the desk. "Now then, what, may I ask, brings you here today?"

"Jessie asked me to come to see you, Mr. Vandam. You'll recall that she recently discussed with you the possibility of the mine owners getting together and agreeing to negotiate with the strikers in an effort to settle things with them."

"Yes, I remember. In fact, I have talked with a number of owners, as I agreed to do, but I'm afraid I have unhappy news to report."

"They would not agree to begin negotiations?"

"They would not."

"Did they say why?"

"They gave the reasons I expected them to give. To back up a bit, I told Jessie when she was here that several

162

important owners are afraid to make a move that's not been approved in advance by Horace Willoughby. Take Virgil Compton, for example. Willoughby lent money to Virge when he badly needed it if he was to stay in business. Virge now refuses to go against Willoughby's position vis-à-vis the strike. As for Otis Delaney, Willoughby is the majority stockholder in Otis's mine, so Otis feels he doesn't dare make a move which might anger Willoughby. I also talked to Barry Barnett, but that was a waste of time as well. As I told Jessie when she was here, Barry likes things quiet and comfortable. He refuses to buck Willoughby because it means endangering the status quo."

"So Jessie is in a position of standing alone on the side of negotiations."

"I'm afraid so. But with one exception. Namely, myself. I'm willing to go along with her and negotiate, although I confess that I hate to give an inch where that firebrand Calhoun's concerned. But I'm no idiot. I can see now that Jessie's position is, in both the short and the long run, the only viable one for a reasonable man such as myself to take."

"Well, that's at least a bit of good news I can report to Jessie," Ki said with relief which was mixed with regret over the fact that Vandam was the only mine owner willing to side with Jessie in the dispute.

"I have to say, though, Ki, that I take my stand with some serious misgivings."

"Misgivings other than your reluctance to give in to Calhoun's demands?"

"Yes. I'm worried about what will happen to the men we have working in our mines at the present time. I refer, of course, to the ones Willoughby arranged to have brought here from Chicago to try to break the strike."

"It looks as if those men will be out of luck," Ki said. "If the strike does end and the strikers return to work, those

163

men will be out of jobs. You certainly won't need two men in a job when one will do."

"I suppose there have to be losers in any situation such as the once facing us, and they are undoubtedly going to be it."

Ki rose and held out his hand. "I'll tell Jessie what you found out, Mr. Vandam. I want to thank you on her behalf for taking the trouble to talk to the other owners."

"It was no trouble at all," Vandam said, rising and shaking Ki's outstretched hand. "Tell Jessie for me that I'm sorry I don't have better news for her."

After leaving Vandam's office, Ki made his way back to the hotel, where he went directly to Jessie's room and knocked on the door.

When he received no response, he knocked again and called her name. He made his way back down the stairs to the lobby and asked the desk clerk there if Miss Starbuck had returned to the hotel.

"Oh, yes, sir, she was here not fifteen minutes ago. I saw her myself. In fact, I gave her a message that had been left for her as soon as she came in. She read it and then left in a hurry."

"Did she leave word for me? My name is Ki."

"No, sir, she left no word for anyone. She just turned around after she read the message and went right back out again and drove away in her carriage."

"Did you happen to see who brought the message for her?"

"It was a young boy, sir. He said he had been paid to deliver it. When I told him Miss Starbuck was not in the hotel, he left it here at the desk and I saw to it that she received it the instant she returned." The clerk frowned. "Is something wrong, sir?"

"No, nothing's wrong." Was that the truth? Ki wondered why he was feeling suddenly uneasy. He decided he was being foolish. True, Jessie usually left word for him if she couldn't meet him as planned. But the fact that she had not left a message for him this time didn't mean anything was amiss. Still . . .

He thanked the desk clerk for the information and went up to his room.

Jessie drove swiftly through the town. She could feel her heart beating rapidly as a result of the excitement she was feeling. *He was free!* She didn't know how he had managed to escape from the stockade or even whether he had not escaped but been released for some reason. All she knew for sure was that Dan Calhoun had sent her a note, telling her that he was no longer imprisoned in the stockade and that he had to see her as soon as possible about something very important. He would meet her, he had written, in the building that housed the Bluebell Mine's stamp mill.

She had wondered when she first read his note and was wondering now why he had chosen the Bluebell's stamp mill as a place to meet. Perhaps, she speculated, he's found out something new about Horace Willoughby's machinations.

Aware of her own growing excitement at the prospect of seeing Dan Calhoun again, and exulting in the knowledge that he was once again free, she couldn't help marveling at her feelings. Where once he had aroused only rage in her, now he had somehow gained the power to arouse other equally potent emotions, but positive, not negative ones.

She could see him in her mind's eye as she drove on. His smooth pale skin that contrasted so dramatically with his curly black hair. His rugged but oddly elegant features and the air of animal-like sensuality he exuded whenever he moved.

At last, after what had seemed like an eternity to Jessie, she arrived at her destination. She drove past the Bluebell's many buildings, heading straight for the stamp mill which, she quickly noticed, was strangely silent. She noticed, too, that no activity was taking place anywhere in the area, although most of the damage that had been done earlier to the buildings was either repaired or in the process of being repaired.

She drew rein in front of the stamp mill and got out of the carriage. The fact that the stamps inside the mill were not in operation, though puzzling, was a relief to her. When such a mill was in full operation, the steady rhythmical thudding of the iron-headed stamps was distracting at best and deafening at worst.

As she entered the building, she could imagine how delighted Calhoun would be when she told him that the lawyer she had hired had agreed to prepare at once sufficient writs of habeas corpus to free every person who had been imprisoned in the militia's stockade.

"Dan," she said, looking around the empty building.

Empty? At this hour? When a full shift should be tending the stamps that pulverized the pellet-sized ore that came from the crushers?

"Dan!" she called out. "Where are you?"

"He's not here, Miss Starbuck," said a rough male voice from behind Jessie.

She spun around and found herself facing Buster. And the Smith and Wesson .44 caliber revolver he had in his hand and was aiming directly at her.

There she is now, Ki thought, as a knock sounded on the door of his hotel room.

"Hey, Jessie," he called out cheerfully. "You don't have to knock the door down. I'm coming. I was just—"

He stared at the woman standing in the hall after he had opened the door, disappointed to find that it wasn't Jessie and surprised to find that it was Matilda Willoughby.

"I asked downstairs," an obviously upset Matilda said, "but they told me she wasn't in her room and for a moment I didn't really know what to do, and then I remembered you from the night we all had supper together at Brother's house."

"Come in, Miss Willoughby," Ki said in a soft voice like the one he would use to gentle a spooked horse. "Please sit down."

Matilda didn't sit down. Instead, she stood in the center of the room, nervously biting her lower lip.

"Is there something I or Jessie can do for you?"

"No—I mean, yes, there is. Oh, dear me, I really must pull myself together." Matilda drew a deep breath and then let it out. "I've come about Brother. I mean, that's why I wanted to speak to Miss Starbuck, but apparently I've come too late for that. She's in danger. Terrible danger. It may already be too late to save her."

"Save Jessie? From what?"

"Buster."

Ki frowned. "What about Buster?"

"Brother sent him to kill Miss Starbuck."

Matilda's words, which had left her lips in a rush, caused Ki to tense. "How do you know that, Miss Willoughby?"

"I overheard Brother talking to Buster earlier today after they had returned to the house from the Bluebell. Brother told Buster that he had had quite enough of Miss Starbuck. He said she was causing him entirely too much trouble, and he wanted her out of his way once and for all."

"Do you know where Buster is now?"

"I'm sure he's where Brother sent him. That would be at the Bluebell Mine. That's where he was to meet Miss Starbuck."

"I don't understand. Are you saying that Buster arranged to meet Jessie at the Bluebell?"

"No, no!" Matilda cried, vigorously shaking her head. "I guess I haven't been making myself clear. I'll try to explain. Brother told Buster to write Miss Starbuck a note and sign Mr. Dan Calhoun's name to it. Then Buster was to pay someone to deliver the note to her here at the hotel. The note, supposedly written by Mr. Calhoun, asked her to meet him at the mine's stamp mill. I suspected when I got here and Miss Starbuck wasn't here that she had already gotten Buster's note and gone to the mine to meet him. Do you know if that is so?"

"I believe it must be because the desk clerk told me Jessie had received a note earlier and that she had then left the hotel in a hurry."

"I should not have waited so long to come here to warn her. But I was afraid. I didn't believe I dared act at first. I have wasted precious time—"

"Thank you for coming and telling me what you did, Miss Willoughby," Ki interrupted. "I'll have to leave you now and try to get to Jessie in time."

"Do you have a carriage? A horse perhaps?"

"No," Ki answered as he headed for the door.

"My carriage is right outside. I'll drive you to the mine."

Ki hesitated. He didn't want Matilda mixed up in the serious trouble he was anticipating. On the other hand, by the time he got to the livery barn and arranged to rent a carriage, assuming they had one available, more time would have been lost, time he knew he could not afford to lose.

"Miss Willoughby," he said, opening the door and hurriedly ushering her through it, "I'll take you up on your offer."

Later, as he drove Matilda's carriage at a furious pace toward the Bluebell Mine with Matilda seated next to him, he said, "There's something I don't understand. When we

168

met for the first time at your home, I had the distinct impression that you were not the kind of woman who would go up against her brother. You struck me as rather meek, if you'll forgive me for saying so. Why then did you try to warn Jessie about Buster and then, when you couldn't find her, come to me?"

Matilda didn't immediately answer the question. She began again to worry her lower lip with her teeth. Then, with a sigh, she said, "That is a difficult question to answer. I'm not even sure I know the answer to it. So much of it is buried in the long dead past. In a mountain of small insults, sneers, bitter actions.

"Even when I was younger, I was not attractive. Polite people called me plain in order to be kind. I was homely then as I am homely now. But, miracle of miracles, I had a suitor once."

Matilda's voice turned dreamy. "His name was Lawrence Tyrell. He was not a handsome man. But he was kind. Generous to a fault. He let light into my rather drab world, did Lawrence Tyrell. We were very much in love and planning to be married. I was full of such marvelous hope for the first time in my life in those happy days."

"What happened?"

"Brother happened. He told me that I was a wealthy young woman, which was perfectly true. He told me that he suspected Lawrence was after my money, not me, not really. I told him he was wrong. But his words haunted me during the nights they made sleepless for me. I began to wonder why Lawrence would want to pay attention to such a Plain Poll as me. In time, quite soon, actually, I began to distrust his motives for wanting to marry me.

"Brother, meanwhile, kept it up. 'Matilda,' he would say, 'watch your step. Don't make a mistake. Don't throw yourself away on a scheming fortune hunter.'"

"I began to believe Brother was right about Lawrence.

So I broke the engagement. Lawrence finally went away after importuning me time and time again to change my mind, to reconsider my decision. He claimed that Brother had poisoned my mind against him. It took me years to realize that he had been right. That is exactly what Brother had done. He scoffed at me later when I said I wanted to study for my teacher's certificate and, when I got it, move to someplace glamorous like Chicago or New York to start a new life for myself.

"'You're not the brightest girl God ever breathed life into,'" Brother would say and smirk. 'What makes you think you can earn a teacher's certificate with your limited powers of thought and concentration? Besides which, why would you want to, my dear Matilda? You certainly don't need the money.'

"Of course, he was right on that score. But, oh, what I *did* need was a life! One of my very own that I could live far away from Brother and his constant habit of crushing every single dream I ever dared to dream!"

"Then I take it your decision to come to the aid of Miss Starbuck was a way of getting even with your brother for what he's done to you down through the years."

Looking straight ahead with an unblinking gaze, Matilda answered, "Yes, it was. At first, when I overheard him talking to Buster, I said to myself, 'Stay out of it, Matilda. This is none of your concern.' That is what I have been telling myself all my adult life where Brother and his business dealings were concerned. Oh, I knew about his habit of establishing assessment mines that earned no one but himself any money, of his fraudulent stock manipulations, and his many other corrupt misdeeds, but I always denied to myself and others that I possessed such knowledge."

"Because you loved your brother."

"Loved him? I *hated* him! It was only today when I heard that he planned to kill Miss Starbuck that I discovered not only that I hated him, but how *much* I hated him! To tell you the truth, I wanted to revenge myself upon him nearly as much as I wanted to try to save Miss Starbuck's life. I know that is a terrible thing to admit, but it is time, I have finally decided, that I started telling the truth instead of living in a cesspool of my own lies, which were the only thing, I now can see, that kept me from killing Brother— or myself."

"I'm truly sorry, Miss Willoughby."

When she said nothing, Ki asked the question that had been on his mind while he was listening to what she had been saying. "Did your brother or Buster have anything to do with the burning of Billy Tippett's house?"

"I don't know," Matilda answered. "But I'll tell you this. I wouldn't put acts of arson past Brother. He has always managed to obtain any and all claims he wanted. He has done so without fail. I have long secretly suspected that he has used, shall we say, less than orthodox means to do so. He may also have ordered Buster to assault that miner whose home was on land Brother wanted—I've forgotten the man's name."

"Josh Ransom."

"Yes, that was it."

"Where is your brother now, Miss Willoughby, do you know?"

"No, but he told Buster he would meet him at the Bluebell to help him dispose of Miss Starbuck's body so that her murder would never come to light."

Gritting his teeth at Matilda's last grim words, Ki drove on, maintaining the furious pace he had established at the outset of his journey toward the Bluebell Mine.

Jessie, taking a step backward, stared at Buster, who had just told her with a kind of muted glee that Dan Calhoun was not in the mill. Understanding suddenly swept over her. "You sent that note to me that was supposedly written by Dan Calhoun, didn't you?"

"Of course I did. I didn't think there was much chance of our plans going awry, because I didn't think it was likely that you'd ever seen Calhoun's handwriting."

"You just said 'our plans.' What did you mean by that?"

"Mr. Willoughby's and mine was what I meant. He's the one what told me to get you to come here."

"Why?"

"I think you can guess the reason if you try real hard."

"Willoughby wants me out of his way."

"He does, indeed, Miss Starbuck. You've been giving him proper fits lately and Mr. Willoughby's not the sort of man who'll stand still for such as that, especially not from a woman, he won't.

"You see, he's afraid, Mr. Willoughby is, that you'll keep cozying up to Calhoun and keep pestering the other mine owners to settle the strike, and the first thing you know Mr. Willoughby will be left out in the cold all by himself after the rest of you mine owners have settled with the strikers for more money and a lot of unnecessary fancy frills down in the crosscuts—"

"I don't call ice chambers and the like 'fancy frills.'"

"Mr. Willoughby does, though. He's a tight man with a dollar, he is, no two ways about it. He's also a man who doesn't take kindly to the idea of you getting in touch with the governor to try to get the militia withdrawn or going to lawyers to get court orders that'll get the strikers out of the stockade. You've been making an infernal nuisance of yourself, Miss Starbuck, as far as Mr. Willoughby's concerned, ever since you showed up here in Cripple Creek."

"So he had you arrange this meeting under false pretenses so you could treat me the way I'm willing to bet you treated Josh Ransom, whose land Willoughby wanted."

"Oh, you're a sharp one, you are, Miss Starbuck," Bus-

172

ter chortled. "I got Ransom alone in an alley one night and I used a club on the unsuspecting fellow. I made sure he knew that the bruises and broken bones I gave him had come his way courtesy of Mr. Horace Willoughby, I did."

Jessie's eyes shifted from Buster and began to roam about the mill as she searched for some way to deal with him. She knew if she tried to draw her revolver, he would shoot her down before her gun could clear leather. She was a fast draw but not, she knew, fast enough to go up against an opponent who already had his gun drawn and aimed at her. Her eyes returned to Buster. "You torched Mr. Tippett's house."

It was a statement, not a question.

One to which Buster gave an eager answer in the affirmative. "I did, yes."

"On Willoughby's orders."

Buster nodded. "Mr. Willoughby needed Tippett's land —the mineral rights under it, actually," he revealed, as if his simple statement explained, and perhaps even justified, his actions. "That's not all the dirty deeds I did of late, neither, Miss Starbuck," he added with a chilling note of pride in his voice.

Jessie waited for him to continue.

"Your mine manager—Fred Bolan. It was me what shot him before you come to town. Oh, I did it on the sly, don't you know? I wanted to make people think it was one of the strikers what did it. To give those boys a bad name, don't you know? And that's exactly what happened. Mr. Willoughby was pleased as punch about that."

"Now you're going to shoot me."

"Not just *shoot* you, Miss Starbuck. *Kill* you would be a whole lot closer to the mark. Drop your gunbelt."

Jessie slowly unbuckled her gunbelt and let it fall to the floor.

"Now, back up. Far enough so you can't make a grab for that gun of yours."

Instead of obeying Buster's order, Jessie kicked out with her right foot and sent her gun and gunbelt hurtling upward through the air.

When it struck Buster, he almost dropped his revolver. He cursed, his gunhand reflexively rising, but too late to stop the missile from striking him on the left temple and drawing blood.

Jessie turned and made a run for it. She kicked a wooden candle box away from the foot of a ladder that led to the catwalk that ran the length of the stamps and then quickly climbed the ladder. As she raced toward the steam engine at one end of the catwalk, Buster let out a roar of rage and fired at her.

She swerved in time and heard the round whine past her left ear and then strike one of the iron stamps with a sharp metallic *clang*.

Her heart pounding, she forced herself to run even faster, her eyes on the steam engine only a few yards ahead of her now.

She heard the sound of running feet behind her and below her. Then she was at the steam engine and switching it on.

The stamp mill suddenly thundered into life as the half-ton stamps rose and fell, rose and fell, pounding down like pestles into the iron batteries below them, which resembled mortars and contained a mixture of water and mercury for the purpose of amalgamation.

The noise drowned out the sound of Buster's pursuit as well as Jessie's ragged breathing. She knew it would keep him from hearing her when she made her next move. Unfortunately, it also kept her from hearing him.

She ran a few paces and then slipped into a narrow space between two of the stamps where she drew her double-barreled derringer from her jacket pocket.

She waited.

But Buster did not appear.

Had he given up the chase so easily? She strongly doubted it. Then where was he and what was he up to? She didn't know and not knowing made her decidedly uneasy. She moved slowly to the end of the passageway and cautiously peered out, looking back the way she had come.

Buster had disappeared.

She stiffened then when she heard him scream to make himself heard over the sound of the pounding stamps.

"Enough of this ring-around-the-rosy, bitch!"

She looked back, and there he was a few feet in front of her. As she fired a shot at him, she realized what he had done. He had gone past her hiding place, climbed a ladder that was just beyond the steam engine, and then doubled back, knowing she was expecting him to appear from the opposite direction.

Her shot missed him.

His shot hit her in the right bicep, causing her to drop her derringer. She immediately bent down and retrieved it with her left hand.

But Buster kicked it out of her hand, and it fell to the floor six feet below the catwalk.

Suddenly Jessie could no longer hear the pounding of the stamps as their overhead camshafts repeatedly lifted and then dropped them into the iron batteries below. The drumming of her own heart now seemed loud enough to drown out their sound.

Time stopped. The world no longer turned. Jessie could hear only her throbbing heart and see only the gun in Buster's steady hand, which spoke to her of death and the end of everything she treasured.

Buster's eyes bored into her own. He took a slow, almost casual step in her direction. His finger tightened on the trigger of his gun. He smiled.

Jessie didn't hear the sound of the shot because of the metallic racket the stamps were making. But she saw Buster spin around, his left hand clutching his right shoulder, his eyes squeezed shut in pain. She saw him stagger and then slump as his knees buckled. She saw him lose his balance and fall heavily to the wooden floor below, his gun falling from his hand as he did so.

Then she saw Ki standing on the floor below her near the spot where Buster had just fallen, her derringer smoking in his hand. She almost fainted with the waves of relief that swept over her at the welcome sight of him.

Then he was climbing the ladder and running down the catwalk toward her. When he reached her, he said nothing. He put a steadying hand on her shoulder and then an arm around her and led her back to the ladder, which he helped her descend.

She had just reached the floor below, her wounded right arm hanging limply at her side, when Ki yelled something. She couldn't make out what he had said, but the look of alarm on his face was enough to warn her that something bad was about to happen.

Turning, she saw that the something bad was Buster, who had retrieved his revolver and was aiming it at her.

She threw herself facedown on the floor. Buster's shot went harmlessly over her prone body. She felt the floor vibrate and saw Ki race past her.

When he was gone, her eyes fell on the wooden candle box which stood near the foot of the ladder she had climbed earlier. Rolling over several times, she reached it, seized it in her left hand, and rising, swiftly advanced on Buster, holding the heavy box against her chest as a shield.

She used it to knock Buster's gun from his hand and

then to hit him on the head with it, dropping him to his knees.

Ki abruptly appeared at her side, her Colt which he had retrieved in his hand. She was about to take it from him when Buster threw the candle box.

It struck Ki, doubling him over.

Buster again recovered his gun and took aim at Ki.

But before Buster could fire, Jessie tore her gun from Ki's hand and fired a snap shot, which hit Buster in the heart, killing him instantly.

She glanced at Ki, who had straightened up and who was staring solemnly down at Buster's corpse, and then started for the door of the stamp mill. He caught up with her, and together they made their way outside to where Matilda Willoughby sat waiting in her carriage.

"Miss Willoughby," Ki said to Jessie, "told me her brother had Buster send you that note that supposedly came from Calhoun. She overheard her brother and Buster plotting to kill you. She came to the hotel to warn you. When she found that you weren't there, she came to me and we drove out here."

"Thank you, Miss Willoughby," Jessie said.

"You're hurt, Miss Starbuck. I'll be glad to take you to a doctor in town."

Before Jessie could respond to Matilda's offer, a carriage came into view in the distance.

All three people turned to stare at it and its single occupant, Horace Willoughby. Jessie's hand tightened on her gun, which was still in her left hand. Matilda's face assumed a stricken expression. Ki's teeth clenched.

"What are you doing here, Matilda?" Willoughby barked as he drew rein moments later and got out of his carriage.

"Why did you do it, Brother?" Matilda asked in a strained voice.

"Do it? Do what? I don't know what you're talking about, my dear. I've done many things today. I've been in touch with the governor to counteract that woman's"—he pointed at Jessie—"efforts to have the militia withdrawn."

He glared at Jessie as he continued: "But the governor, despite my efforts to persuade him to do otherwise, has ordered the troops withdrawn by the end of the week. Hot on the heels of that unhappy news, I received word from General Bell that the lawyer she hired"—he pointed again at Jessie and gave her another withering glance—"arrived at the stockade less than an hour ago armed with writs of habeas corpus, which have resulted in the immediate release of all the people General Bell had taken into custody."

Jessie felt joy surge within her at the news that Dan Calhoun was free again, but it quickly faded as she thought again of what Willoughby had ordered Buster to do to her. Turning to him, she said with undisguised pleasure, "I'm taking you to the sheriff in town."

"You're—surely you're joking!" Willoughby exclaimed, but his eyes were darting nervously here and there.

"If you're looking for Buster," Jessie told him, "don't waste your time. He's dead inside the stamp mill, where, following your orders, he tried to kill me just now."

Willoughby blanched. Then, recovering himself somewhat, he declared, "Miss Starbuck, you are being preposterous. I did not order Buster to kill you. Such an accusation is patently ridiculous."

"Is it? Before he tried to murder me, Buster told me he was following your orders and that you were going to meet him here to help him dispose of my body. It's obvious to me now that you shut down your mine for the day so that there would be no witnesses to the crime you and Buster planned to commit."

178

Willoughby chuckled. "Can you prove all that? You just told me Buster is dead, so he certainly cannot corroborate your accusation against me. Thus, he cannot testify against me in a court of law."

Matilda said, "It's true, Brother, that Buster cannot testify against you to prove that you were an accomplice before the fact to murder," Matilda said harshly. *"But I can."*

Willoughby glared at his sister. "What are you talking about?"

"I heard you order Buster to kill Miss Starbuck, that's what I'm talking about. I went in search of her to warn her about your plot against her."

"Matilda," Willoughby said, his voice a weak bleat, "you wouldn't—you couldn't—"

"What have I ever done to deserve such treatment at your hands? I've always—"

"You've always belittled me," Matilda interrupted. "You've always treated me with scorn and contempt. Murdered all my hopes and all my dreams just as you tried to have Miss Starbuck murdered here today. That's what you've done to deserve the truth from me at long last, Brother."

Jessie raised her Colt and leveled it at Willoughby. "I'll ride back to town with you in your carriage," she said. "You'll drive us to the sheriff's office, where I intend to press charges against you."

Willoughby, his hands fluttering helplessly in front of him like two wounded birds, looked from Matilda to Jessie and back again. "Matilda!" he cried in a cracked voice. "Don't do this to me. Please, I beg of you. I'll change. Things will be different from now on. I know I've been remiss at times in my relations with you. But I'll remedy that—at once. Matilda?"

His sister, an implacable expression on her face, ignored him completely and drove away.

"You can drive my carriage back to town, Ki," Jessie suggested when Matilda had gone.

"You'd better see a doctor once you drop Willoughby off at the sheriff's office," Ki advised, and Jessie promised to do so.

As Ki drove away from the mine, Jessie, her Colt firmly in hand, marched Willoughby to his carriage.

Late that same day, after Jessie had left Willoughby in a cell in the sheriff's office, visited a doctor to have her wounded arm treated, and paid a call on Cornelius Vandam, she arrived in the lobby of the Nugget Hotel to find not only Ki waiting for her but Dan Calhoun as well.

"Ki told me you had been shot," Calhoun said after greeting Jessie. "I would have killed Buster for hurting you if you hadn't done the job already yourself. Are you all right now?"

"I'm fine, Dan. It was only a flesh wound. But what about you? The stockade—"

"Well, the food they served was far from the best and the accommodations left much to be desired, but overall I survived the place without too much pain or travail."

Jessie found Calhoun's smile both heartening and seductive. "I have some good news for you, Dan. Some potentially good news, at any rate."

"I'm always happy to get good news. What's yours?"

"I stopped by Cornelius Vandam's office on my way back here and told him everything that had happened earlier at the Bluebell. He told me he's almost one hundred percent certain that the other mine owners will now agree to negotiate an end to the strike since Willoughby's out of the picture. Vandam told me earlier that Willoughby had a hold of one kind or another on several owners. That hold is now broken so—"

"Happy times are here again!" Calhoun cried, clearly exultant.

"Well, they may not be here just yet," Jessie cautioned him. "I have a feeling there is going to be some tough bargaining ahead for both of us."

"But at least there *will* be bargaining, which is a whole lot more than we've had up until this point."

"Jessie, you've got more company," Ki interjected.

She turned to find Fred Bolan and Alan Sanders hurrying into the hotel.

"Jessie!" Bolan cried when he saw her. "I heard you were shot. Are you all right? What happened?"

"Bad news surely does travel fast, as they say," Ki observed after which Jessie told Bolan and Sanders what had happened at Willoughby's mine.

"So Buster was the one who shot me," Bolan muttered when Jessie had finished speaking. "I'm sorry it's too late, now that I know that fact, to repay the man in kind." He shrugged. "But let's put the bad news behind us," he suggested, brightening. "Let's talk about some good news that Alan and I came here looking for you to tell you. Go ahead, Alan. Tell her."

"Miss Starbuck, that process I told you about," Sanders began breathlessly, his eyes glowing.

"I believe you called it your cyanidation process."

"That's right, I did. You gave me the go-ahead to try it out on a larger scale than my original small experimental one. Well, I did that, Miss Starbuck, and I'm happy to tell you it works just fine."

"Wonderful! Congratulations, Mr. Sanders."

Bolan said, "We processed an entire ton of tailings, Jessie, and we extracted from that supposedly worthless material gold worth, on today's market, nearly two thousand dollars!"

"Why, that's amazing!" Jessie exclaimed, almost as

breathless now with wonder as was Sanders. "Then the process is worth putting into place at the Empire on an even larger scale."

"That's right," Bolan affirmed. "Do we have your permission to do so?"

"You not only have my permission, gentlemen, but also my blessings."

"Then, if you'll excuse us, Miss Starbuck," Sanders said, "Fred and I will get right to work on it."

"That's certainly going to increase the overall profitability of the Empire," Ki commented when the two men had gone. "Immensely," he added.

"It's also going to do something else," Jessie mused thoughtfully. "It's going to provide a lot more jobs for miners here in Cripple Creek, which, in turn, means that the process can put the strikebreakers on the payroll together with the men who have been on strike when the negotiations end. Mr. Sanders's cyanidation process has just given us the chance to give a job to everyone who wants to work."

"I have to tell you I'm glad of that," Calhoun declared. "I'd never have admitted it before, but the thought of men like Josip Tito and his friends being thrown out of work once my men went back to work in the mines never gave me any pleasure."

"Do you two want to come with me?"

"Where?" chorused Ki and Calhoun.

"To Mr. Tito's to tell him the good news. But, come to think of it, I don't know where he lives."

"I do," Calhoun announced. "He and some of his friends took lodgings at a boardinghouse on the south side of town. I can take you there."

When the trio arrived at the boardinghouse, they were shown to a room on the third floor. Jessie knocked on the door.

It was opened by Lena Tito. "Yes?"

"Miss Tito," Jessie said, "we've come to have a talk with your father. Is he here?"

"Something it is wrong, yes?"

"Something is not wrong," Ki told Lena with a smile. "In fact, something is very right. Now, where's your father?"

Lena stepped back and they entered the large room beyond the door, where Josip sat on a mohair sofa.

When he recognized his visitors, he sprang to his feet.

"Mr. Tito," Ki said, "we have some good news for you. It looks like the strike is almost over."

"That is not good news. That is very bad news, my friend. It means I have no work when strike is over. My friends, they have none, too."

Ki hurriedly explained about Sanders's cyanidation process and what it would mean to Josip and the other men who had been brought to Cripple Creek as strikebreakers. "So there will now be enough work for everyone who wants a job," he concluded.

Josip's face brightened and he began to smile. He seized Lena, lifted her off her feet, and swung her around in a circle.

"Papa!" she cried, laughing. "Put me down!"

Josip did. "Miss," he said to Jessie, "I go now to my friends with this good news you bring to me. Is all right to tell them it, yes? Is not a big secret?"

Jessie smiled and said, "No, Mr. Tito, it is not a big secret, and, yes, you may tell anyone you like about the new cyanidation process."

Josip, excusing himself in both English and Serbian, hurried from the room.

"I thank you for this," Lena said to Jessie. "Papa, he was worried about what would become of us all when strike is ended as he said it must do someday. Now we have good jobs to look forward to in future."

"We'll be going now, Miss Tito," Jessie said, and started for the door.

"Not me," Ki said.

When Jessie gave him a quizzical glance, he explained, "I haven't seen Lena in some time, and I thought I'd stay and get reacquainted with her. We had just started to become friends when I lost track of her in all the subsequent excitement."

"See you later, then," Jessie said, and left the room with Calhoun.

As he closed the door behind them, Jessie said, "Well, Dan, we have a great deal of business to attend to, you and I. We have our first negotiating session to plan and then—"

"Did I ever tell you my favorite motto, Jessie?"

"No, what is your favorite motto?"

"Pleasure before business," he answered.

Jessie took his arm and squeezed it.

Watch for

LONE STAR AND THE ARIZONA GUNMEN

91st novel in the exciting
LONE STAR
series from Jove

coming in March!